WORDS AND WOMEN:

TWO

2015

CAMEO

First published in 2015
By Unthank Books
www.unthankbooks.com

Printed in England by

All Rights Reserved

A CIP record for this book is available from the British Library

Any resemblance to persons fictional or real who are living, dead or undead is purely coincidental.

ISBN 978-1-910061-15-2

Edited by Lynne Bryan and Belona Greenwood

Cover design by Rachael Carver

CONTENTS

Preface

– Sarah Ridgard –

The metaphor of short stories as being tiny windows into other worlds and minds and dreams is attributed to the writer Neil Gaiman, who goes on to liken stories to journeys which can take the reader to the far side of the universe and still be back in time for dinner. And indeed the Words And Women prose competition encouraged almost two hundred women writers from all over East Anglia to do just that, to set their unique journeys down in words and submit a diverse array of fiction and non fiction. They presented a glimpse into places across the globe, from the Caribbean to South Korea and India, from America to coffee shops in Norwich and the sand dunes on the north Norfolk coast.

As exotic or local the location, however, what dawned on me as I read through the longlist of submissions, was how much I yearned for the unusual. Motherhood, relationship difficulties, terminal illness, these were frequently written about, in some cases skilfully so. Yet despite the writing being careful and controlled, all too often these pieces fell flat and slid through me without touching the sides. Some lovely writing in parts was ultimately let down by the unoriginal premise of the story.

It was equally frustrating to read prose that was working away at a different idea but where the writing wasn't strong enough to get it off the ground. So it was the work which had an originality to it, both in the voice and its ideas, and was raised to another level by wonderful writing, that leapt out of the pile. Lora Stimson's *Cornflake Girl* was such a story.

Intriguing and captivating from the first sentence, the writing in this story is so delicate, so pared down, it reads as if were set down fully formed on the page (though I imagine it probably wasn't). There is a beautiful restraint to the narrator's voice as she tells her story and a humour which underlies the writing

9

throughout, even as a quiet depth charge is launched in the middle of the story and the damage becomes apparent to the reader. For me, it's a near pitch-perfect piece of writing that quietly opens a small window onto what it is to be human.

There were other entries that rose swiftly to the surface, including Melinda Appleby's *Footprints on the Tideline*, an elegant and insightful piece of nature writing in which the writer meditates on her relationship to the north Norfolk coast she knew as a child; and *Kurt Cobain's Son* by Julianne Pachico, a story about fame and idolatry in which the dialogue and humour is written with such verve, the reader gets swept along at speed to the end. These were among several submissions that made me want to read beyond the story, to look at maps of the Norfolk coast and locate Seahenge; to google fan fiction, look up images of Korean bulgogi and find out more about the 1984 Sikh massacres in Delhi.

Then there was the very funny and engaging *Game of Love!* by Holly McDede which unpicks the games that people play in relationships, and the rather beautifully written *You Have What You Want,* Anthea Morrison's moving reflection on the shifting sense of self and ephemeral moments in early motherhood.

A reader once remarked at a book group I attended a few years ago, that the novel under discussion, really only came alive for her upon reading it for a second time. She was able to work out the threads of the story, how they all connected, and picked up on the nuances in the writing that foreshadowed events in the book. The book was all the richer for it, she said. A few people in the group, going by the look on their faces, were no doubt thinking they'd struggled enough with the first read and couldn't contemplate a second...*too many other books to get through... life's too short.* However, the woman explained that her second reading of the novel wasn't unusual as she read every book twice because authors who had put that much effort into a book deserved a commensurate effort on the part of the reader. It was only decent and respectful, she said, to those writers she chose to read.

I was mindful of that reader as I read and re-read the longlisted work, all of which had been read carefully already by the Words And Women organisers, Lynne and Belona. More often than not, it was the work that yielded more on re-reading, the writing that revealed further depth and an original take on the world, which won a place on the shortlist.

So as subjective as all judging is, it's the process of reading, often by several people, that makes writing competitions such as this, so valuable for any writers serious about their work. It's a chance to have our work read and demand sufficient attention to be re-read and, we hope, to be rewarded for our efforts.

I'm sure it's frustrating for many writers when a prospective agent/editor/ reviewer labels their work as 'quiet' (I can't be the only one?), as if that's a reason in itself to stop reading, that a piece of writing can't have anything important to say unless it's a little bit more showy and obvious. In choosing the winning story, *Cornflake Girl*, and many of the other entries included in this anthology by talented writers from all over the region, I hope we can prove a point that writing can be 'quiet' and be all the more intelligent and profoundly moving for it.

Editors' Note

– Lynne Bryan & Belona Greenwood –

The majority of the texts in this anthology have been selected from entries to our 2014 prose competition, four however originate from another competition entirely...

In August 2014 women writers based in the East of England were invited to submit a proposal for a short text of 4,000 words or half an hour long exploring the life of one woman and her relationship to place. The woman could be famous or not, contemporary or historical, fictional or factual. The place had to be within the East of England. The text could be in any form - a script, prose, poetry - or a combination of forms. It was a very exciting call-out and we had no idea what to expect.

We wanted to create an opportunity for the development of new texts about strong female characters and to set this writing in this part of the country. It was very important to us to feel as if these stories could only take place where they were set. In other words, the environment dictated how the story developed and was a character in the telling. The project was experimental. We were looking for texts that would be a good read on the page and yet make strong performance pieces.

The About project was funded by Arts Council England and supported by Writers' Centre Norwich, The Forum in Norwich, and Unthank Books. There were four paid commissions and a mentoring programme. The aim was to include the texts in this anthology and to perform selected extracts on International Women's Day at our launch event.

Fifty writers entered our open competition judged by Words And Women, theatre director Adina Levay, performance poet Hannah Jane Walker and Andrew Cowan, Director of Creative Writing at the University of East Anglia. The proposals featured swimmers, vagrants, mothers, clubbers, writers, prostitutes, teenagers, witches, a composer, a lepidopterist, an ecologist, even a station mistress. Many concentrated on historical figures. The most popular locations were Norwich and Cambridge, although the coast featured heavily and The Broads. The difficulty of living in isolated small communities was a frequent theme.

The judges found it extremely difficult to select their four winners and twelve commended writers. Most of the entries had been developed with great care and imagination.

Jenny Ayres, Lilie Ferrari, Tess Little and Thea Smiley, our four winners, attended the first of a series of Saturday mentoring sessions in October and November 2014. The workshops marked the beginning of an endurance test in writing, shaping, drafting and redrafting the texts. Our writers were amazing and demonstrated endless patience, resilience, skill and talent. Lynne Bryan of Words And Women and Hannah Walker took on the task of editing the work for print, but publishing the texts has only ever been half the story. The writers had the choice of performing their own work at our launch event, or being a part of the staging process with actors slipping into the characters' roles. All four pieces were rehearsed and directed by Adina Levay, with Belona Greenwood of Words And Women, in a series of workshops held in February 2015.

It has been a privilege to be a part of creating new writing that is strong, compelling and true, and to work with the writers who have given new voice to the silent, marginalised and lost.

Kurt Cobain's Son

- Julianne Pachico -

When I was thirteen years old I was best friends with Kurt Cobain's son. We met at summer school, or what everybody called Nerd Camp—even the people that went there. The class we took together was called Parallel Universes and had lots of really good books on the syllabus, some of which I'd already read (*1984, Brave New World*) and some of which I hadn't but had definitely heard of *(Moby Dick II: The Great White Return)*. Day one, we had to go around the classroom and say our names, favorite book and an interesting fact. When it was my turn, I said without hesitating that my favorite book was *The Fountainhead* (I'd just finished it) and my interesting fact was I loved to write fan fiction.

'Thank you; that's great,' the teacher said, at the same time that one of the boys in the back, Isaac or Ian or somebody, said, 'You love to write *what?*'

When it was Kurt Cobain's son's turn, he sat up a little straighter and folded his hands on top of his desk, as though this were a truly formal occasion. He said his name was Andy and that his favorite book was *The Hitchhiker's Guide to the Galaxy*. 'Can you get back to me about the fact?' he said, looking at the teacher and blinking slowly. 'I need time to come up with something excellent.'

'No problemo,' said the teacher. His name was Ryan, or maybe Brian— they were always pale graduate students, those Nerd Camp teachers of ours, instructors of Introductory Compositional Writing in Midwestern states, places famous for their crops of corn or potatoes or other vaguely yellow vegetables.

I knew he was Kurt Cobain's son right away. It wasn't just his last name or the fact that 'Andy' was clearly a reference to Andy Kaufman, his father's favorite comedian. I knew it from how he looked, with those big blue eyes and shaggy blond hair. I knew it from his skinny wrists, from the way he'd inherited his father's crippling stomach condition, which explained why his cafeteria lunch tray was always loaded with bowls of steamed spinach and mashed potatoes. Bland-tasting foods, pale and mushy, while the rest of us overloaded on everything we were never allowed to eat at home—Lucky Charms, chicken wings, frozen yogurt with all the toppings. I never heard him mention his family, but this one time in class, he made a comment about how 'back home in Seattle' his grandma always made him put sunscreen on the insides of his elbows so that they wouldn't get burned on rare sunny days.

I talked about him with all my friends. Right before biting into a corn dog, Haylee said that was why Kurt had first gotten addicted to heroin, you know—to deal with the chronic stomach pain. Walking back to the dormitory, Sarah-with-an-H wondered if Andy was a Pixies fan, just like his father. Spitting toothpaste into the sink, Carolyn said that Sean Penn had helped Andy move into the dorm on the first day—her dad had run into them on the stairs. Sean Penn had been holding a box of books in one arm and an empty laundry basket full of ramen packets with the other.

'Of course it would be someone like Sean Penn helping him move in,' Carolyn said knowingly, turning on the faucet. 'Instead of someone like Morrissey. And of course Sean Penn would only need one arm to carry a box of books, instead of two.' She spoke too loudly, Carolyn did—her voice echoed off the tiled walls and bounced off my eardrums as I hid in the stalls, tremblingly waiting for everyone to leave so that I could finally pee in privacy.

Sandra Bullock's daughter had come last year, and rumor had it that a pair of twins, descendants from the Hershey's Chocolate founder, also attended. But this was different. Kurt Cobain was someone we knew. Someone like Kafka or Michael Stipe or Kurt Vonnegut (the other great Kurt, arguably the greatest of all). Someone whose lyrics we scrawled on the last pages of our school notebooks, whose face gazed out from posters plastered on our bedroom walls back home. He was someone that mattered.

We first spoke at the dance. Everyone was grinding to Destiny's Child, hips moving expertly and whooping, as I slunk towards the gym entrance. I found him just as the DJ was starting to play Van Morrison's 'Brown Eyed Girl'. He was sitting on the edge of a potted plant and using a Liquid Paper pen to decorate his hiking boot: head bowed, intensely focused. I stood behind the door, chewing my shirt collar, until one of the Resident Advisors touched me on the elbow and asked kindly if I wanted to help her refill the Tootsie Roll bowls on the snack table.

'No problemo,' I said. As we walked away I turned around to look at Andy one last time; he was starting to work on the other boot.

We spoke again a few days later at Cloudwatching, the Mandatory Fun activity I'd signed up for that afternoon (Mandatory Fun consisted of obligatory afternoon activities, every Monday through Friday from 3-5pm; the other options that particular day were Bracelet Making, Killer Cardio Abs and Holler for Soccer). I lay down on the grass, close enough so that I was near but not exactly next to him, and watched him play cards with the only friend I ever saw him spend time with, Dan from Miami. Dan had a lip ring and had once read aloud a story in class about visiting a Disney-themed suburb where his grandmother lived. Right now Dan and Andy were talking about the just-released remake of *Moonstruck*, in which Cher and Nicolas Cage reprised their exact same performances with the lines unchanged.

'The film is all the more poignant and melancholy now that they've aged,' Andy said, shuffling the deck. The Liquid Paper on his boot spelt out THIS MACHINE KILLS FASCISTS in wavy letters, like a horror movie poster. 'Plus Cage's performance is so much more Oscar-worthy in this version.'

Dan nodded as he selected a card. I agreed as well, nodding my head vigorously and tearing enormous clumps of grass out of the ground.

There were a couple of other instances. There was the time he read his short story out loud for Workshop, a rollicking adventure set in an alternative universe filled with tuxedoed waiter fish, bohemian poet hedgehogs and angry banana peels. When he held up his notebook to show the cartoon drawings he'd made to go along with the text, I thought, *We are going to be together forever.* Another time, during Quiet Writing, I sneaked a peek at his journal page. He was carefully printing out the lyrics for The Clash's *London Calling*, one song after another (he'd just finished 'Rudy Can't Feel'). The back of my own notebook was filled with the lyrics I'd memorized from *Jagged Little Pill*, including instrument credits and linear notes. I thought, *Our children will just love this.*

And then there was the time we went to downtown Baltimore. The Resident

Advisors walked us there, thirty minutes from John Hopkins' central campus, so that we could spend the afternoon poking around in the second-hand shops. I found the poster of Kurt Cobain in the music store, hanging in the back. It was that famous black and white photo of him, the one that appeared on the Rolling Stone cover commemorating the anniversary of his death. Holding an acoustic guitar, shaggy hair hanging in his eyes, head bowed, intensely focused.

I took the poster to Andy, heart pounding in my throat.

'Hey,' I said, tapping him on the shoulder. 'It's you!'

The poster crinkled against my torso as I held it open. Andy only glanced at it for a second before looking straight at me.

'Fuck you,' he said. He didn't move, didn't even break eye contact, until I backed away.

There was an anthology reading for the creative writing classes that year. I was chosen to represent our class and got to read my story in front of all the parents. It wasn't a fan fiction piece this time, not even a disguised one—I don't remember what it was about. What I do remember is right after the reading, when I was racing towards the bathroom, I nearly collided head-on with Sean Penn, who was coming up the aisle and drinking a Jamba Juice. Maybe he stopped and said something. Maybe he just kept walking. I ducked behind a pillar and hid there, eyes lowered and face bowed, and waited to see what would happen next.

Lucky, Lucky Girl

- Sarah Baxter -

My wardrobe has an old-fashioned pullout rail, even though it is nearly new and made from white melamine. I rifle through layers of coats and finger a broken plastic button on the sleeve of my parka, remembering five years ago – the last time I pinged the coat from its wire hanger.

There had been a free music festival in the local park. The parka skimmed my bare knees. Underneath I had worn a navy tea dress, spattered with ditzy white flowers. I'd scrunched my skinny feet, with their odd-bod long toes, into leather sandals.

That was the midsummer of the mad rush towards each other - all we'd done since February was eat good food, drink bad wine and fuck.

The music had already started when we arrived at the park. A college band, whose audience consisted of doppelgänger scruffy lads and teenage girls dressed like me, only with more authenticity, raised their plastic pint glasses in the tinny chorus.

I asked Mark to find me some wine from one of the stalls. I twirled into the crowd, making space among the college kids as they danced around grey hessian rucksacks, etched with Sharpie pen strokes. I thrust my hands into the parka's deep pockets, head down, singing in the circle of myself.

Halfway through the concert, clouds the colour of a petrel's wings rolled over the stage. Sheets of rain split the crowd. Onlookers threw themselves towards the edge of the arena, huddling under the striped canopies of cupcake vendors and knickknack stalls.

My coat darkened and wrinkled, clinging to my thighs. Mark appeared. I grabbed his hand, dragging him under the long lashes of a willow tree - safe and dry, wombed in green.

I kissed him and tasted yeast.

'Where's my bloody wine?' I'd asked.

'Sorry, I forgot,' he replied. 'Is this your secret den?'

'Sort of. I used to come here for a smoke and a snog on the way home from school.'

'Grammar school girls were the worst,' he laughed.

'Not me. I was a good girl.'

'Let's see if you're corruptible now.'

Mark wrapped his arm around my waist, pushing me against the tree's trunk, easing my dress upwards. He pinged my knicker elastic until I thought it would snap and I'd be under a tree, my dignity sagging between my knees.

'No one's looking,' he said.

'Don't!' I cried, when I really meant: Do. Do.

I pulled away, skipping backwards through the willow's curtain into the rain. I raised my face to the volcanic skies, stretching my parka to make a bat's wings in the hurly-burly.

Then I didn't exist for three weeks.

The first thing I saw when I returned to the light were helium balloons sagging above my head: Get Well Soons bobbed at half height, no longer straining against their ribbon tethers; Happy Birthdays floated higher because they were newer. These were signs left behind by visitors – some tokens of hope for my recovery, and others guests at the thirtieth birthday party I didn't have.

Mark told me it had happened so quickly. One minute I'd been spinning in the cloudburst and the next I'd been twitching on the ground, eyes rolled so far back that all he could see were their whites.

I was a lucky, lucky girl. Wild current had stopped my heart, but Mark had scooped me up and sprinted to the St John's Ambulance tent.

I would thank them later, the volunteers who didn't stop pounding, even when my ribs cracked, and the paramedics who restored my whump-ga-gump with tame electricity, after it had stopped.

I thanked Mark too. The nurses said he'd sat by my bed for twenty days and as many nights.

I let go of the parka's button. I shrug on a cocoon coat made from boiled wool by a Danish designer – so smart, the Danes, so angular, so far from the days of tea dresses.

I push up the coat's sleeves leaving my hands bare. Since the lightning chose me my hands are hysterical with pain. The doctors can't explain it. They say the strike hit me under my left breast, drawn from heaven by an underwire, and discharged through my right foot. My hands were only witnesses, not participants.

I have tried pills, but they don't deaden the pain. They move my head further away and make me feel waxy. The only cure is winter's chill. I can't tolerate my hands being touched, or touching myself until December's solstice. Mark says I should try.

Today is cold enough; a fashionable coat with short sleeves will do as well as pills.

Mark kissed my eyebrow before he left for work – his little thing, his trademark kiss.

'Are you sure you don't want me to come?' he said.

He was already wearing his cycle helmet. I pulled the duvet around my neck and shook my head.

'OK. Give me a call later. Be good,' he said over his shoulder.

And then he was coats-on-and-gone, believing I was headed to the city for a follow-up appointment with another specialist about my treacherous hands.

It's a greasy November morning. Thin rain springs up from the platform, imparting a lick-spit sheen across my forehead. I jump onto the 10:12 with a day-return clamped between my lips.

I take a seat at the rear of the carriage and the doors beep-beep-beep. A jowly salaryman tests the toilet door, poking it open with his elbow. He squishes himself into the cubicle's interior.

I unspool my iPod and jab in the white earbuds. My local hospital is under special measures for something-or-other and so my GP referred me, and my new pebble-hard lump, to a London hospital without question. I don't care where I am seen, only that it can't be at the same hospital I was blue-lighted towards five years ago, for reasons I don't understand, only feel.

The salaryman bursts from the toilet, pushing my knees aside with his shins as he slings his laptop bag into the luggage rack. He slumps down heavily. The alkaline glaze of toilet scent lingers. I glance at his hands: *I hope that's water,* I think.

But I do not think, I say. My words bully themselves out. The salaryman chokes and gives a stupid nod. He wipes his hands on his lap.

I spend the rest of the journey with my mouth tight-shut, enduring the man's jiggly leg against my thigh, while strings of Sibelius sing in my ears.

The hospital's thrum fills the entrance hall. A sparrow-faced receptionist, her blonde hair scraped into a ponytail, takes the letter from my outstretched hand.

'"Clip thirst,"' clucks the woman, 'that's unusual. It's mostly gobbledegook.'

'Sorry?'

'The letter. There's a password in case you want to change your appointment online. You've got "clip thirst". Real words.'

She gives a triumphant smile and turns to her colleague: *Look, aren't I clever with my observation.* Her ponytail takes an exaggerated arc. The swish is a shade lighter than the scrape of hair against her scalp. It shines too hard - acrylic, not the natural stuff.

My cue to comment: 'Of course, real words.'

'Follow the red line all the way to Oncology,' she replies.

Oncology. Now that's a real word.

There's a racetrack of coloured lines painted on the polished floor and a sign at the beginning of the corridor with instructions matching the colours to the maladies.

The red line for Oncology is flanked by a blue line for the X-ray department, a yellow line for Orthopaedics, and a green one for Audiology - broken bones, bent bones, lumps and eardrums. The red line stops at the bottom of a flight of stairs. The other lines peel off at right angles, like a bad rainbow.

The waiting room for Oncology is as I imagined - a pastiche of gathered objects, set out as a lounge. The plump vinyl chairs circle a low coffee table, stewn with well-thumbed magazines: Top Gear for him; OK for her; Classic Boats for god-knows-who.

There are two people sat at opposite sides of the table. A man in his fifties, stares vacantly, a floral handbag across his knees. The corners of his mouth turn up a smidgeon when I open the door, then fall back. A woman, perhaps my age, maybe older, wears a headscarf, knotted at the front. She is reading a book - one I haven't heard of, not a bestseller.

'You've come prepared,' I offer, sitting next to her.

'Yes,' she replies, without looking up.

My name is called. I am thankful. There are no friends here.

I sit on an orange plastic chair, the type unstacked from cupboards in village halls for community meetings, as the consultant goes through test results and makes his proclamation. A nurse blah blahs, spooning out optimistic leaflets. She tries to take my hand, but I pull away and rub my fingers along the moulded edge of the chair until I start to feel.

Clip - to cut, to curtail. Thirst - a sense of dryness in the mouth, a desire. I am to be curtailed. They'll cut me and zap me with docile radiation. They'll ignite my veins with savage heavy metals, but it won't be enough. And what of my desire, what of that?

I leave the hospital and stalk towards the High Street. I mooch around the chichi second-hand shops selling vintage blouses with stiff, ochre-coloured armpits, as if all I have is time to kill. I spend daft money on a mulberry cloche with a pert feather. I ignore the phone when Mark's number flashes up. I ignore it eight times.

He's on the 6.23 - the same salaryman. *What are the chances?* his eyebrows say.

Better than average - there are six trains an hour after five o'clock. Our evening meeting is a thousand times more likely than a lightning strike, even if the clouds were provoked by a balconette bra worn by woman grasping for something she'd lost. Even more likely than a bundle of cells misbehaving in the same breast the bra had thrust skywards.

29

I sit down next to the salaryman and smile thinly.

The train heaves out of the station, taking me home to Mark.

I will cook dinner and we will sip wine. And when the bottle's empty, I will press my furious palms against Mark's chest and tell him I have been chosen again.

Footprints On The Tideline

- Melinda Appleby -

You look back across the years of landlocked life,
Call up the voice of redshank and curlew,
Drift down across sea lavender and samphire,
Walk again through dune and marsh
To the tideline, where you left your childhood.

The sand is firm, warm, salt scented. Sanderlings scuttle before me, picking at strands of seaweed, running ahead like busy lawyers. It is September, at the point of the full moon, and a spring tide so high it had slipped up the lane to the village. Now it is retreating, sinking low into the northern horizon so that, on this shallow shore, there is a mile of abandoned sandbars, pools, shell banks and an ebbing sheet of water.

I am walking west along the Norfolk coast, a shifting network of marsh, dune and creek. I am retracing my footprints from childhood. This is where I grew up; where I learnt about moons and tides, seasons and cycles, life and death. Behind me, the sea swirls sand into my prints, erasing them, removing evidence of my path. Have I left a memory if not a mark? Some cultures believe that, even after people have gone, something of them remains where they have walked.

Old Ordnance Survey maps mark this coast with the words 'Ancient Forest'. That it was here, submerged, was not in doubt. I had, as a child, collected peat pebbles, gnawed and rounded by the sea; broken them apart to find the shreds of plants still inside. At times the sea scoured out the beach, digging into old mud banks where brown crabs sheltered from sunlight, revealing the old forest floor. It was a series of just such destructive tides that, in 1998, exposed a wooden construction that became known as Seahenge.

A chance find of a Bronze Age axe, and the subsequent emergence of an oval enclosure of wooden posts, triggered investigation by the Norfolk Archaeological Unit. The 'henge' consisted of fifty-six oak timbers with their bark preserved on the outside, leaving the impression of one enormous tree. Sheltered inside was an inverted stump, also of oak, reaching down into the earth, its root shield looking up to the sky. There is increasing evidence that some prehistoric sites, including Stonehenge, are aligned to the midwinter sunset and Seahenge had two timbers creating a narrow gap with this alignment. The construction has been dated to the early summer of 2049 BC.

Before it could be claimed by the sea forever, heritage experts and archaeologists prepared a plan for its excavation and removal. But other groups, such as neo-druids, wanted the 'henge' to stay put, to face an uncertain future of reburial or erosion. There was heated emotion on all sides. The archaeologists won. The timbers were removed and shipped across to Flag Fen, East Anglia's prime Bronze Age site. After treatment, they were relocated to Kings Lynn's museum as a permanent exhibit.

The conjecture around Seahenge focused on the central upturned tree. Had it provided a place for excarnation, here on this liminal site, haunted by gulls and crows? The last resting place for a body to be picked clean by birds; for the soul to be released by the removal of flesh? In mythology, the tree links heaven and earth with its roots in the underworld and its branches in the sky. Celtic people, it is believed, venerated the oak, whereas Scandinavian cultures chose the ash. It seems strange to ponder a connection to the oak, standing on a wind-swept, treeless beach.

Seahenge was built on the edge; a land of forest and fen looking out across the North Sea. But at one time Norfolk was joined to Europe across a vast fertile plain known as Doggerland. This was largely submerged by 6500 BC, due to meltwaters from glacial ice sheets. It is slowly giving up information as fishing vessels and wind farm developers trawl artefacts from the sea bed. These suggest an occupied land, where people would have roamed as tribes of hunter-gatherers. We cannot understand their culture, their association with the land or their beliefs. We can only surmise that they would have been concerned about the gradual loss of their hunting grounds, and that the forest must have begun dying from salt incursion. The legacy of this huge landscape and its loss may have carried on in oral histories and given rise to myths of spirits dwelling under water.

Walking along this tideline, empty of people, I see recent evidence of the changing coast. Field drains from when the land was cultivated before the 1953 flood; concrete gun emplacements and pill boxes from the Second World War. Constantly eroding and rebuilding, dunes disappear and marsh creeps over sand. Growing up here, a place touched by man but still retaining its elemental wildness, I learnt respect for the sea, for what it brings and what it takes away. I saw how the moon, when full, pulled the tide up the beach and then sucked it out to the horizon. Some days the rotting planks of old wrecks were revealed, sticking up from the sand like the bones of a lost animal. As the tide oscillated, it shaped and sculpted, left its signature in skeins of bladderwrack, cast off mermaids' purses and discarded starfish.

I walk past the site of the old 'henge' beneath the shadows of pine shelterbelts. Tucked into dunes, in an old war time bunker, is the Holme Bird Observatory where I once helped record the annual autumn migration. It still runs a ringing programme, capturing, recording and releasing the many birds that pass through this migrant staging post. It is a magical experience to sit on the dune ridge in September, and watch birds tumbling down into the sea buckthorn after a long flight. Fieldfares, redwings, finches, even robins and owls, all streaming in across the North Sea.

I walk out further to Gore Point. The tide is still dropping. The Point is a triangular ridge of hard sand that runs west towards the Wash. It can be completely submerged, but twice a day, the whole area is deserted by the sea and left as a rippled, salt strewn, unpeopled place. Knowing the time of the tide, I am fairly certain of my safety. I walk on. The sand is shell-less, paddled over by gulls and laced by threads of sea lettuce. Away to my right, the sea is sinking below the horizon; to my left, are the marsh pools and dunes between Holme and Hunstanton. The flat landscapes in East Anglia, particularly at the coast, provide a 360 degree distant horizon of sky, sea and land edge. Our prehistoric ancestors would have looked around and up at the sky. Circles within circles.

I walk further out into a salt sand desert. I become as small in the landscape as a Borrower beneath the floorboards. The gulls grow large. I am in their element. I feel disconnected from my world. I see no-one and smell only the sea. The gulls laugh at me as they lift into the onshore breeze. I stop and take a circular view.

Alone on a sandbank; all the horizons hazy. A distant light playing on water, a mist shimmering over land. It is now I feel fear. How long since I left the shelter of Holme beach? How far to run back if the tide turns? The wind carries the calls of birds mocking me; sand whips round my ankles. I turn and retrace my footprints. I am stepping back through the glass, growing in stature as the sea fades away to a tideline.

Reaching the safety of Holme, I cross a shallow ripple of water. A redshank pipes out of a creek, the air smells of mud. I can hear the sea, like a constant breath, *whooshhh aahhh, whooshhh aahhh*. It never stops. I retrace my steps past the beach, emptied of its 'henge', wondering if the energy of the land has been changed. Where once the upturned tree reached into the underworld, now only a shelf of sand and mud remains. When it was removed, did the tree take with it our connection to the past and erase the memory of our ancestors? What would they think of it now, housed out of context in Kings Lynn's Museum? I feel compelled to offer something back, something of myself. With a razor shell, I describe a circle in the sand. Within the circle, I make a firm footprint.

And now it is time to leave. I take off my shoes in surrender to the open beach and run along the tideline. The sand is damp, clinging to my heels. Freedom comes in the wind and the feeling is elemental, old. Behind me the sea puddles in my footprints. I am a child again.

Shaddup

- Lilie Ferrari -

Court of Quarter Sessions, Norwich Guildhall, 1631.
Accused: Jane Sellars. Theft.

My heart is going thump thump thump wooden wheels over cobblestones.
Thump thump thump. Wooden wheels.
Carrying a cartload of strangers to the Weavers Hall.

Shaddup, Jane!
No I won't! Why should I?

In my mind trouble started when they come to the city. Before the strangers
everyone in the business had work my dad says. City was known for it.
Weavers hosiers spinners fullers shearmen.

There was that big hall down St Edmunds Coslany. Dyeing everything.
Purples reds yellows greens. You've never seen such colours. And all the boys
doing the dyeing. Dozens of them all with stained hands where they dipped the
cloth in the vats of colour and dyed their own skin.
Me I've known a few of them. I'll tan your hide if you do the deed with one of
those boys my dad would say.

Oh yes. There was one. A very toothsome boy. Tom something….. Thomas….
Tom Barker. By Christ. Yes. Tom Barker. He had green fingernails like a goblin
or a sprite and green…. Well. Look here at these little emerald stepping stones
climbing up my leg.
Try explaining that to your –

Martha Johnson. Come up now.

So. Martha is at the stairs. Head up. She's not afeared. Courage Martha.
Door crashes closed again and we're back in the dark.
Thump thump thump.
Martha going up the steps to the court.
My heart with her.

So. The strangers come. And that boy? He ends up no trade all the dyeing work
going to the strangers. And those strangers they work all night if they have to
just to finish a job. Norwich boys wouldn't do that they've got better things to
do with their nights.

Jane, shaddup!

Better things to do with their fingers.
He's on a ship now.
On his way to the New World.
Taking his gentle creeping green hands with him. Tom Barker.
Lizard fingers slithering up another tree on the other side of the world. I could
have – never mind.

The sun rises the moon wanes and we get on with it don't we? No use thinking
about what might have been that's what my dad always says.
Said. What my dad said. He died did I mention that?

Snow cold down here. And there's too many of us in a bitty space. The other
prisoners are dirty and belching and foisting don't make for a pleasant odour
and mostly drunk. I wish I was.

Court of Quarter Sessions, Norwich Guildhall, 1631.
Note to Judge presiding: Accused has appeared before the Mayors Court
fourteen times between June 1623 and this day, found guilty variously

of living idly; being vagrant and out of service; petty theft; ill rule; lewdness; begging. On May 1ˢᵗ of last year, the child of Jane Sellars was put to the wife of Matthew Grove of St. Swithins to be kept. Jane Sellars has appeared before this court prior to this day, and found guilty of various felonies, including the theft of a ruff worth ten pence; six pairs of stockings worth eight shillings; the theft of a linen bodice, two shirts and two smocks; the theft of an apron and a smock.

Nowhere to sit so I am hunkered on my haunches.
Tell the whore next to me to pack up her pipes stop bawling at me to shaddup when she's making more noise than ten thunderstorms put together.
Me I'm just wanting to tell my story and she's wanting to blaspheme enough to wake the devil.

So. Are you listening?

Back when I was a girl. Guild day eighteenth of June as I remember.
So I'm at the New Mayor's Gate in Tombland with Jenny Bensley Anna Barlow also known as Chicken-Face and Chicken-Face's mother who we're trying to get rid of as we want to get ale and when you are eleven and being followed by someone's mother the getting of ale can prove tricky.
It's been a marvel of a day.
We've been to the fair we've lifted a few things from the market nothing big. Bit of lace. Ribbons. Just poke-shakings in truth.
We've gone up the castle mound and rolled down skirts wound tight with the ribbon so no-one can see our drawers.

Rolling over and over the world all sideways sound of horses and people and laughing and a flash of sun and then earth in your nostrils and then round again 'til you get to the bottom in a big heap…

And now the moon is up and they've lit the torches and there's music playing and people dancing in the castle meadow and Mother of Chicken-Face has got lost in the crowd and the people!

You can hardly move for the bodies against you but it's alright because everyone is laughing and there's the hot smell of ale-breath faces grinning down at us and we're happy and eleven years old with all our cares before us and none behind.

After that it's all darkness and my breaking heart.

It's the fireworks like it always is every year for guild day only this time – fireworks breaking away into the crowd – hissing and bursting flames and screaming and people running every which way.

We climb up to the window sill of a house on Magdalen Street to stay out of danger. Because you can see people below can't breathe and they're going all blue.

Up on a ledge little canary in a wooden cage trilling its head off in the window. They must have been Dutch in there they like yellow birds in cages don't ask me why. But they do sing a treat.

Thirty three died in the crush.

One of them was my dad.

I didn't even know he'd gone to the fireworks.

Had a bellyful of ale because he'd just lost out on a big passel of work lost out to them strangers which meant his face was dark and furious and he shoved me almost into the fire when he heard.

Then out he goes and don't come back.

Three days it was before my grandmother went to the Parish and found him laid out his face all stove in.

She knew it was him by the black toes where a horse once stood on him.

Although the Beadle said everyone dead had the same feet because they had all been stood on in the crush.

But my Nan said she gave birth to him she'd made him his first shoes she'd changed his diaper cloths knew his feet as well as she knew his face.

So.
That's what happened to my dad I think.

Chicken-Face always said she heard he had been pressed into service and someone seen him going up a gangplank at Yarmouth docks a week after the guild day firework disaster.
She can think what she likes.
I want to think of him fambling on about the strangers then he knocks back a jug of ale brings a smile back to his face maybe dancing on the cobbles with some tart who takes his fancy then – whoosh.
Can't breathe.
Gone.
Out on a high note.

Not drowning in some foreign sea or lashed to the mast of some ship being beaten by some bastard with gold braid on his jacket.
Trying to be brave my dad but frit inside. Wondering about his Jane and what the hell will happen to her.
Shall I tell him now? Tell him I'm still his girl always will be and when we meet in Heaven there will be such times and laughing.

Jane Sellars a-crying! Not a sight I seen before.
Tears like water in the Wensum.
Tears is no good, Jane.
And don't you start a-wailing.
You'll soon be up before those wiggy gentlemen, Jane.
And they'll frown at you same as the Magistrate.
And they'll order you a whipping same as they always do.
And they'll send you to the Bridewell same as they always do.

Only I'm colder here than I am generally.

And I'm bitty fearful to tell the truth. And I'm bitty weary of trying to pull myself up and being pushed down.

Silly sod.
Your back's so rough now you won't feel the lash hardly.

Light comes sudden and they shove in a man shape and just before the door slams shut I see Robert Morgan from the Bridge Tavern.
Put here for housing vagrants in his upstairs rooms. They said they'll have his ear off if he does it again. I can just see him in the darkness clutching at his earlobe like if he holds on hard they can't have it.

Mister Morgan is that you?
Shaddup, Jane, some of us are trying to catch some shut eye.
Heart is heavy like a hog's head.

Martha has not come back down.
Where have they sent her?
Am I to follow?

It's the bad old judge, Jane Sellars, he'll have you up the ladder for sure.
Hanging judge, Jane.

So I'm fifteen years old when the next thing happens. I think. Borned two years before the king was crowned.
So.
I've gone with Jenny Bensley to see the priest's head on a pole at St Benedict's.
His quarters are on four of the other gates but it's his head we want to see.
Grey it is all lead colour and sad.
Died because he believed something about God that was wrong. Changed his religion. Maybe he thought he'd see Paradise if he changed sides but that face — it didn't look like it saw anything good on its way out.

Anyway I get home and there's my Nan with the same grey face stretched out on the mattress.

Mouth open like she's fallen into one of her half-dead sleeps.

But after a bit when she don't get up and wobble on her stick legs to stir the pot I go over and shake her and then I see. She's wobbled her way out of this world entirely.

Gone. And now I'm on my own.

Must make my own way in the world.

Because the Strangers come and took up the worsted weaving and that put an end to my dad.

Strangers did for Nan too. She just was a sad thing after Dad and never smiled again.

But after I cry a bit and Nan's put in the Pauper's pit and covered over Jenny and Chicken-Face take me to an ale house and things don't seem too bad.

The city looks after its own.

This is my city.

Norwich.

Safe inside its walls.

My friends my neighbours – they'll care for me - that's what I'm thinking because that's the way it is here.

Door opens light comes in and they push some old fambling pugnasty down the steps and she lands right next to me and puts her horny crabbed fingers to my face feels like a dry old toad.

Jane Sellars!

I don't know her name but I seen her at the gaol in the Mayor's Court done for lewdness.

Jane back here again! You're a nizzy, girl. Lucky they don't put you in the dark house, for you'd have to be mad to keep a-coming back here.

As if I choose this life! I want to say: *godsookers, woman! You think I steal because I want them things? You think I stay here because I want to be put to the post? You think I have this mark on my hand to show I am proud of what I done? You think I am not pigsick of the Bridewell and dogsick of the lash and cowsick of the life I am made to lead?*

She stumbles over to the bussbeggars' corner and starts up singing and I have to put my hands over my ears to shut out the sound which is like the Devil's choir.

I know my city.
Think.
Yes.
Safe inside the city walls.
I know my city.

I can tell you how to get from St. Peter Hungate out to St. Giles under the city wall. Round the corner by the pump down the alley past the old woman with the shrivelled legs who sits on her arse begging outside the Rose Tavern then under the low bridge by the farrier's – you can't miss it because of the horse stink and then down the cobbles all the way to the wall. And that's me who can't read or write I just learned the way. Though why anyone would want to go to St. Giles is beyond me.

My dad says you must make your own way in the world because no other bastard is going to step in and assist.
In short if someone asks me to help him find St. Giles and I happen to be standing a bloody mile distant on the other side of the river in Fybridge I should tell the bugger to sod off unless he wants to show me the colour of his purse.
So I find my own way.

And the place I usually find myself having made my own way is inside the Bridewell and my little Susan some other place finding her own way.

The Bridewell was never where I aimed to be but then my dad would say that life has a habit of sending you places you didn't expect.

But I think he meant Yarmouth or Lowestoft.

So I am in the city once more in the dark pit of the Guildhall gaol.

Norwich yes so that's a good thing isn't it as this is my home.

Am I in a good part of Norwich?

No.

And am I weary sick of the Bridewell where they will send me again?

A dozen times, Jane!
Twelve times, Jane!
Thirteen times, Jane Sellars!
Look at her, a-weeping like the Candlemas Flood.

Maybe fourteen times at least I've been done for something and ended up in that sorry hole and it doesn't get better with age.

Neither do I.

Babby Susan is somewhere better I'm pleased to say.

I hope she is.

I don't mean Paradise. They said they sent her off to be with a wife of St. Swithin's Parish. But why couldn't little Susan be with her proper mother which is me.

I would have made Susan a good girl. I would have done anything so Susan had a life not like mine.

That face of hers she will be a proper beauty that I know. But who will save her from this life if I cannot?

It's not far. Bridewell is Mid Wymer. St. Swithin's is West Wymer next door.

When I come out of here I can go and find her follow the streets I know to her door. Peek in the window. See if the wife is looking after her like she should be. They say she gets paid for it.

If they paid me to look after Susan I wouldn't have been scrubbing floors in the Bridewell for nothing would I?

They whipped me hard that time and the leaning over with the bucket and the brush it make my back scream. Sores won't heal. Biddy on the palliasse with me dabs at them with her hanky every night and prods the bits that are bleeding. Not much of a help but she means well.

You mean Biddy Whitney?
She's gone, Jane. Took down by the ague.
Long gone.
Gone for good, this time.

The Bridewell is not a place you would want to call home. It's always cold like I am now. Cold like death.

A place for shivering like this place.

Like my grandmother's skin when I touched her after she went.

And yet it seems I must keep returning to these holes low down in the ground with small windows and no sunlight.

Blackness.

Biddy would ask me why I love the City when it don't seem to love me. Because I can see the sky above the church spires and I know it carries on up and out there maybe to Heaven and maybe to my nan and my good old dad.

Jane Sellars, shaddup, will you?

The magistrates in the Mayor's Court say I am a bad girl and now I am to go before the judge and the jury at the Guildhall court where they have a verdict decided by men of property.

I am going up in the world.

It's the hanging judge up there.
Start your prayers, Jane Sellars.

The priest comes visiting while I'm in the Bridewell and says the perfect state
for a young woman is to be married.
But who will marry a girl who is given a bad name the way I am?
I ask him that and he slaps me for having a shrewish tongue and tells me to
mind my manners or no man will have me.
He has a terrible wart on his chin with a hair sticking out of it.
No wonder he's a priest for no woman would think to marry him which I'll
wager is why he is so angry all the time.
With my cheek still stinging from the slap I smile at him my nicest smile and
show him a little taster of my swollen babymilk mubbies and he huffs away
pretending to be right full of disgust but I've known enough men to understand
what means that little mound rising beneath his gown and I smile again at his
leaving.

In truth my teeth are my best feature.
Just two rotten among the lot of them.
It's the raw potato keeps them shining.

Smile won't help you in here, Jane Sellars.

It was the fault of Mr Day. That man is a jumbler. Plants his nog wherever he
can find a hole to put it.

I know the truth.

And if there is the man upstairs as my dad calls him then He knows it too.
Although I'm a bit less inclined now to believe in that upstairs place and the
man in charge no matter how many times they push me to my knees and make
me pray.
But that's a thought I'll keep to myself.

God's a good man they say. I'm beginning to surmise that he's a right old sod like most men. Except for my dad.

Call for the priest, Mister! There's an old buzzard perishing away down here!

It's dark as the inside of a cow in here. Just shapes looming and then back down again. Some rotting old crones are gathered round a bundle of rags and the bundle is coughing fit to burst.

Herc, herc.
Shaddup, old witch!

There's a law says if a master has a household he must pay for everyone in it. But there's no law says that if a master pulls a girl into the wash house and does the dirty deed and walks away like it's nothing buttoning up his pants like he just took a piss and then the girl finds her monthlies not arriving and is in a panic and tries to hide it and then tells the cook what happened and she tells Mistress Day who doesn't believe a word of it although she knows it's not the first time and Mr Day tells me himself all grey in the face like a dead man that I am a bad girl and he'll have no more of me - that law doesn't happen to exist.

The three old bussbeggars near me keep shouting for the constable. Don't know how they still earn coin from doing the poop-noddy with punters. Hardly a tooth between them and riddled with the pox and smelling of piss.

And the shape on the ground coughing still but quieter now.

Herc, herc.

Like something stuck in her throat.
They are singing now but they are afeared too. We all find our own way to stand tall in the darkness old slaplardies.

Shaddup, Jane!
I will not!

I'm got rid of by Mistress Day and back out on the road so I come back here to the city where I feel comfortable and stay with a widow who lets me do a bit of carding to keep the wolf from the door and stands over me mouth open like a dumbskull when Susan starts coming.
But I mustn't be angry with her she gave me a roof when no other human would and afterwards I carry on the carding with Susan in my lap a good babby sleeps most of the time or at the breast supping like there's no tomorrow.
And then I don't mind the soreness of my mubs and the blisters on my fingers from the carding because the lonely lonely feeling of being by myself has gone there's my girl now and I don't care if her dad's a cockscomb that won't make her a bad person.

My dad beat me sometimes when he'd had too much to drink and he'd say evil things to me when he was tired but I still knew that I was his best girl and when he was happy he'd call me the light of his life and that's what I say to Susan in the deep dark night when I hold her close and smell her warm baby sweat.

That Mister Henry Day he don't know what he's missing.

I am the winner out of us both.
Him with his lemon lipped Mistress Day and his servants and his carriage and his buckskin shoes and his three dogs.
And me with sweet Susie.
She don't look much like Mister Day to be truthful.
She look more like that that Dutch boy I dallied with once when I was in service with the Days.
Peter his name was.
Not Walloon.
Dutch.
From a place called Rotterdam by the sea that is between his land and ours.

Blue eyes like the sky on a Spring day. I remember that.

The missus had gone away to Peterborough with the master so I was at liberty in the city. And there is a pretty Dutch boy smiling at me in the alley.

Peter.

But I had so much to drink that night I can scarce remember if we made the beast with two backs as they say or what.

Peter Heybaud.

A beef-brain.

A booby.

A bufflehead.

No. I would have remembered.

So I'm with the widow and we do well enough considering she has no teeth and I'm fond of a raw potato.

But then the widow is prosecuted for lodging a masterless young person which is me and I'm out again.

It's because I am so young and I damn them for it.

Is it my fault I am only twenty and some years?

They are all nokeses angry because they are old and not free as I am.

As I was.

I went back to the widow's lodging the last time I was at liberty but she had gone and the neighbours not willing to say where.

My guess it was the pestilence and she's upstairs in Paradise with a comfortable chair and a big pot of soup on the fire for her to dip her bread and mash with those soft old gums and a horsehair mattress to rest her weary old bones.

She was a proper Christian soul even if she did smell a bit. Jane Sellars she would say you are a good girl take no heed of them that say otherwise. Stealing when's necessary is not stealing in truth. God smiles on the needy she would say.

I miss her flim-flammery I do.

Call for the priest, someone! There's an old bussbeggar dying over here.
Shaddup down there!

You are to stay in the Bridewell 'til you be retained in service that's what the
Beadle said. Only he knows as well as I that there's no service to be had.
They train you up spinning and weaving and bobbing your head and scrubbing
and scouring so you can go out and be a slave in some smart household.
Only trouble is – there are too many slaves and not enough households.
They give you a fortnight to find yourself work then when there int any and
no-one wants you they arrest you again for being idle. Put you to the post and
make free with the birch cane to open up all the scabs that just healed.
Then here you are like you've never been away.
Back on the palliasse with Biddy and the fleas and no babby allowed here so
Susan has to go.
You see?
Making my way in the world only the world int so friendly as I'm finding out.

They brand me on the hand so the whole city knows I've been needy.
Flames of hell on my upturned hand.
They hold it in a vice.
A deal of pain for me to tell people what God already knows.

And the anger inside me I must keep pressing down because a girl with a sharp
tongue is scorned by all men and cutting words will never get me a husband
which seems to be the only answer like the priest said.

If the King was crowned when I was three year old which is what my
grandmother always said – or was it two year old? - then I am three and twenty
when they first take me and stand me in the Guildhall and tell the Magistrate I
have been found idle at Trowse. He is a fearsome looking gentleman much as I
imagine God to be and frowns at me and pulls at his wig and asks me if I have

anything to say to prevent my being put away.

I tell him my story.

I am working in the fields picking strawberries with Chicken-Face and her
mother only the rains come bad that day and we're laid off and Mother Barlow
and Chicken-Face go off in a cart because someone says they can help with the
harvest at Whitlingham in the morning and sleep in a barn.
But I stay to dunk my head in the water from the millgate because I am
scorched by the sun having no decent bonnet to stop my neck from burning
and that's when the men come and take me up no matter me explaining that I
am hired at Whitlingham.

It was bad luck. Us being born under a black star like Dad used to say.

Because I was standing on the Norwich side of the millgate so they could take
me up and bring me to the magistrates.
If I had knelt the other side they would have left me there for not being part of
the city.
Black star or sod's law that was how they got me the first time.

So that being a part of Norwich was my undoing and being a part of Norfolk
and outside the city complete I would have been harvesting with the Barlows
and a few coins in my pocket for the alehouse that night.

It's hard to love Norwich sometimes.

The magistrate made out he was listening but someone was talking in his ear the
whole time and he was nodding at them and pointing to a paper on his bench
and when I had finished he said to put me to the post and then the Bridewell
having no family to speak of so he hadn't heard a word.
Him and God both –

Shaddup, Jane Sellars!

And after the Bridewell they give me a paper all covered with words tell me it's my pass out of the city show it at the gate and be on my way.

Only I don't want to go as this is my home so I use it to wipe my arse in the privy midden best place for it and turn back down an alleyway to try my luck in the city again.

Court of Quarter Sessions, Norwich Guildhall, 1631.

December 12, 1631. Court of Quarter Sessions. Jane Sellars. Accused that between eight and ten of the morning of 21 November she entered the house of Elizabeth Abell and stole items to the value of twelve shillings. A woman's ruff, a linen bodice, two pillows, a handkerchief, a neck-cloth....

Come on up you pair of tatmongers!

Two more girls are taken up the stairs and I hear the bolts go back across the great wooden door and now at least there's room to breathe even if the air is full of damp and if I put out my hand I can feel little rivers of sweaty slime sliding down the walls and it smells like the very devil still.

The bundle of rags has stopped moving and is making no sound.

But a drab in the corner is weeping and crying for her mother a terrible wailing 'til someone slaps her and she falls silent.

My mother died of the pestilence when I was but two or three year old the Lord have mercy on her soul.

My dad says we are lucky to be alive although it's a funny kind of luck takes your wife away and leaves you with your toothless old mother and a baby.

But Dad says life is a gift.

And my mother is in Paradise which they say is where you go if you have been good.

Which is a worry.

If only I had my little Susan to hold close and to feel her sweet breath against my ear and to know she is happy and safe and sometimes thinks of me.
I call her Susan Sellars. I do not want her to be Susan Day.
Or Susan Heybaud.

They say the Strangers get farthing tokens as alms if they be poor.
And what about the English poor say I.
A few more farthings and I wouldn't be where I am now and babby Susan with me.

I went into the house because Anne Bensly who I thought to be my friend bade me do it. She said she could sell the things and we would share the riches.
November it was. Freezing cold the wind whipping round the corners and fair to knocking you off your feet and me with only my grandmother's shawl a grey and sad thing thin and weary like my grandmother.
Truth be told I could have got myself a new coat if Anne Bensly had not been a liar.

December 12, 1631 Court of Quarter Sessions.
….a woman's cloak, a tunic, a smock, an apron, a petticoat, a diaper napkin, a printed box and two pieces of linen.

She knows this Mistress Abell who is a merchant's wife and lives near the castle in one of those tall red houses with the chimneys which means they have more than one fireplace which means money which means I can have a new coat.

And she says there's a door near the dairy which they never lock and where I can get in and she says *she* can't go because her bad leg will slow her down and I'm so small and dainty I can squeeze in a corner should someone come and I'll be out of there before the stable boy comes for his milk and no-one the wiser because even if he sees me the boy's a dumbskull and will think me a friend of the mistress.

And she says that the mistress always goes to a neighbour's at nine of the clock to drink a bowl of tea and so I will not be interrupted.

And to take whatever I can find best pickings in Mistress Abell's bedchamber which is up the stairs which is where I go and what I do.

And the one thing she forgets to mention is that Mistress Abell has a dog a slanty white-eyed thing all black and curly with a red tongue and small ears like the Devil like no street dog I have ever seen.
And it barks and barks and barks even though I kick it.

And someone comes and I am caught.

I am outside the gate and I throw the things to Anne Bensly but she won't reach out.
And then the servant comes and takes me hard by the arm.

And Anne Bensly says she never met me before in her life.

<u>Norwich Court of Quarter Sessions, Guildhall, 1631.</u>
Note to Judge presiding: Anne Bensly accused of receiving said property and tried in this court Tuesday last. Found not guilty.

My dad says you keep your chin up and you look the bastards in the eye and you don't never say you're sorry.

The door above me opens and the light is suddenly upon me and faces turn my way.

Go on, Jane Sellars!
Move your stumps, Jane.

The man is waiting for me now. I am to go up now.

Stir yourself, girl. Court is waiting.

Light is right in my eyes. I stand up blinking and blinded and smooth my skirt
as best I can. Hold that head up.
They won't see me looking afeared.
And I take a step forward into the sun dazzle towards the door.

Norwich Court of Quarter Sessions, Guildhall, 1631.
**Jane Sellars convicted of theft. Sentenced to death by hanging in the
Castle ditches at a date to be decided. No chattels.**

Little Susan with her blue eyes like the Spring sky.
Nobody writ down what happened to me.
There's only Susan to carry on in my name.
And all I can do is talk.
Say things.
Keep saying them' til the darkness cloak is over me.

Wooden wheels over cobblestones.
Norwich sky bright and fair.
Up to the castle mound and soon I will be rolling down into the ditch.

I say we was alright 'til the strangers come.

Camera Black

- Hannah Harper -

What I've learned from watching Mark is who he is when he's alone. Little things I might not ordinarily have noticed. For example, he jiggles his right foot on a base spoke of his swivel chair constantly when he's at his desk. He's doing it right now. He scrapes around the insides of his ears with his little fingernail, inspects whatever matter he manages to accumulate, and then flicks it onto the carpet. I have never seen him do this in my company.

If I ask him what he had for lunch he always says, 'a sandwich'. But this doesn't even begin to describe the process I'm watching. First, he gets the wooden chopping board from the draining rack, together with the cheese slicer and two knives – an ordinary dinner knife and a sharp, slim little knife he uses to cut the sandwich in two. Then he goes to the fridge and gets out a block of cheese, margarine, some kind of meat product (greasy slices of chorizo, wafer thin prosciutto, mustard infused ham) and occasionally cucumber. He does this fast, and when he leans over the ingredients, a lock of dark hair always falls onto his forehead and my fingers tingle to brush it away. Sometimes I brush the screen instead, tracing my index finger over him, making the picture ripple slightly under the pressure.

He takes two slices of bread and brushes the left slice with margarine. The meat product always goes on the margarine, and the cheese on top, sliced into thin rectangles with the cheese slicer. Cucumber, when he uses it, goes over the meat. Now he presses the two halves together, neatly cuts the square in two, and places both sides under the grill, on the highest setting, for two minutes. He times this by his watch. While the cheese is melting, he'll make a cup of tea, bag straight into the same blue mug, brewed until the timer for the sandwich goes off. Then he'll carry the plate and the mug over to the glass-topped table in the corner of the kitchen. I'll watch him eat. The camera allows us to have lunch together, even though I'm in the office and he works from home. I can study him in a way I can't at home. I can zoom in on his jaw, admire the way it tenses and relaxes as he chews.

He used to masturbate at his desk, although he hasn't done that for a little while now. I watch him on his laptop, writing away. I'm at work, he's at work. I can tell by the expression on his face when he shuts down for the day how it's gone. In this way, I am always in the right mood for him when I get home. If his day was good, I'm cheery and chatty. I'm more measured if it was frustrating. We're always on the same wavelength. It's part of what makes us work.

My phone rings – someone has been put through to me by accident. I deal with the call. When I put the phone down and return to the screen in front of me, what I see makes me stand up so fast my chair shoots away. I lean forward, palms on desk, sickness rising. I can see two people moving about in my kitchen. Except only one of them belongs in my kitchen. It's Mark and a woman, a shiny blonde woman, holding a bottle of wine. A woman with her hand on my partner's back, a light touch but familiar, knowing, she's priming him. And he's making more sandwiches. He's made an allowance for her. He doesn't want me to come back for lunch, ever, though I'm only a short drive from home. He never wants me to share lunch with him. But for this woman, it's fine. She gives him the wine, his eyebrows rise in happiness, he wraps her in a hug. He kisses her on the cheek. Now she's laughing, tipping her head back, one hand on our kitchen counter, cool fingers on marble, the other on her hip. And how is he behaving? He puts the wine in the fridge. He continues his routine for her but he is sloppier in the delivery. He spills crumbs, he talks and chops, he gestures with the cheese slicer. She gets another mug from the cupboard and makes herself some tea. Who is she and what are they talking about? He hands a plate to her. He's having lunch with this glossy woman he's never mentioned and he's keeping it a secret from me. As I rack my brains to remember his manner this morning, last night, they sit at the little glass table in the corner like conspirators and chat earnestly. Not for the first time, I curse the lack of sound. I'm squinting, nose practically to the screen. I throw my lunch in the bin.

My boss taps at the window and pokes her bony head round the door. I minimise the screen and try to smile.

'Knock knock and do we need to get you an eye test?' She raises an eyebrow and rolls my chair back along the floor to me. 'What are you working on that requires nose to screen viewing?'

She has never asked precisely what I am working on before. I feel myself blush. If she asks me to show her my screens, I'm dead. But she doesn't. She says, 'Relax!' as though it's funny and rambles on about nothing while the precious minutes tick by. Then she says she just popped in to discuss the Riley bid and can I prepare a debrief of my progress for her tomorrow.

'Of course,' I say, 'of course.'

He reappears, alone. He clears away – he washes up their two plates, two mugs. But instead of leaving them out on the draining rack, he dries them with a tea towel and puts them away. I watch him peel some potatoes and put them in a pan, covered in cold water. That means he plans to surprise me later with sausage and mash – one of my favourite dinners. I am a lucky woman. I do know how lucky I am. He spoons the slithery skins straight into the bin afterwards. He is neat, just like me.

It's been snowing. Some people find this exciting: I'm not one of them. I just need to get home to Mark. At five thirty on the dot, after shutting down my computer and switching off the screen to save energy, I change from my suede court shoes to wellies, and trudge through the smudged white to my little car.

It's only a short journey home, a twenty minute drive if the traffic is good. But because of the snow, the roads are completely gridlocked. To try and control my rage, I pretend I have a business colleague in the car who I have to impress with my cool-headed thinking. I glance over at the passenger seat.

'How about this?' I say. 'This is all we need.' I switch the radio on. 'What's your station?'

'How about the traffic and travel news,' I reply. 'It might shed some light on what's going on here.'

I continue in this vein until I see someone in the car opposite looking at me strangely. So I touch my fingers to my ear, to make them think I'm wired up to the hands-free.

It takes me two hours to get home. Two fucking hours. I get frantic, thinking about Mark. When I'm with him, I'm absolutely fine – as cool and calm and full of love as anyone is when they're with the person they were made to be with. But when I'm not with him, it's different. Tonight, for instance, I sit in my car, staring at the way the streetlights reflect off the snowy roads, watching pedestrians slip and slide along, and I think to myself, what if he gets tired of waiting for me and just leaves? Crazy, isn't it? Usually I worry he's online, flirting with others, making intimate connections from our home together. Or I worry he is going to leave me for the attractive barista who works in our local coffee shop where I know he sometimes sits with his laptop when the words aren't flowing at home. Today, of course, I have a more immediate concern – the blonde woman, the blonde with wine, the blonde who laughs and hugs and eats his sandwiches. My heart is pounding. I scream out loud and slam my hands into the steering wheel. I accidentally beep the horn. The person next to me mouths something. 'We're all in this together.' No we aren't, I think, no we fucking aren't.

I finally get home and Mark greets me with a kiss, as he usually does. I hold onto him more tightly, though, I linger in the kiss, I try to put my tongue in his mouth.

'Later,' he smiles, kisses my hair. 'Caught in the snow?' He looks excited. His eyes glimmer, his cheeks are flushed. I tell him about the drive, ask how his day was.

'Cracking,' he says, but he doesn't elaborate. I am in agonies of knowledge. 'How was yours?'

'Oh, you know. Same old same old. Lisa wants a debrief tomorrow morning of something I haven't done yet.'

'How come you haven't done it yet?' Mark asks. I'm surprised. I think he finds it boring to hear me talk about my work. Usually he doesn't ask for further information.

'I don't know, really,' I shrug. 'Busy doing other stuff.'

'Got lots of other projects on?'

'A few.'

He gives me a look I can't read and goes to get the plates from the oven. He loads them up with my favourite dinner and puts my portion in front of me.

'Wine?'

I start. I flush. I look at him; he is smiling down at me. 'Ooh, why not?' I say, trying to be light hearted. 'That's a treat on a week day! What's the occasion?' This time I don't look at him as I ask. Instead I concentrate on the sausages. My mouth is dry and I feel sick.

'No occasion,' he says, setting the bottle of white she brought on the table between us. So: it is official. He is hiding her from me. The bottle is so cold there are beads of condensation on the body.

I concentrate on the sound the wine makes as it fills the glass. 'Did you nip out 'specially?'

'I might have done.' He winks at me.

Just before we switch off the light to go to sleep, we always cosy up together. Tonight I force myself to do the same, although I'm surprised he can't hear my heart beating through my skin. We face each other, warm under the duvet, knees touching, and put our noses together, and chat for a little while.

'You smell nice,' he says.

'It's my face cream.'

'Well, it's nice.'

We're quiet for a bit, and then he says, 'Love is a funny old thing, isn't it?'

'What do you mean?'

'I love you and yet I have no idea about you.'

'Yes you do. Of course you do. Silly.' I laugh.

'You could be thinking anything, in that brain of yours. Anything at all. I wouldn't know.'

I snuggle up to him. 'The only thing in my brain is you.'

He laughs and switches off the bedside light.

I am in work early, very early. I have to write this debrief before my meeting with Lisa. I try not to switch on the camera screen, I try so hard. I wait for my computer to load, I open only the relevant documents, I begin typing notes on the bid I haven't worked on, basic notes to orientate myself. But my finger is drawn to the icon, it double clicks, and soon the familiar picture appears. My living space with Mark. I flit between screens, zooming from work to home, waiting for him to show. And as I flick from spreadsheet back to kitchen, suddenly she is there again. Waiting so patiently by the boiling kettle, so at home, waiting to make two cups of tea. Here is Mark, back on camera, and he is carrying a chair. A chair? Why would he be carrying a chair into the kitchen?

His body looms near as he places the chair beneath the high row of cupboards which house our glasses, mugs and cereal bowls, and my body knows before my mind what he is about to do. I clamp my hand over my mouth, biting back a scream. Then he looks me directly in the eye, and puts his hands up to the camera – and it goes black. The camera goes black.

Then there is nothing more to see.

You Have What You Want

- Anthea Morrison -

The bedroom window is open, but there is no breeze to bring the cooler air of night into the room. The duvet lies in a heap where she kicked it off earlier, covering clothes she has not put away, books she has not read. For the third, fourth time tonight – she has lost count - she gets back into bed and pulls the sheet over her naked legs, shifting them to find a cooler patch of the mattress. Silence. The relief of the rapid fall towards the soft escape of sleep.

The cry reaches her when she is still on the way down, spinning her into consciousness. She sits up and puts her face in her hands. She too wants to cry but finds she is too tired. Instead, an unfamiliar numbness settles over her. Automatically she swings her legs off the bed and crosses the landing again. Moonlight is seeping through the curtains, reflecting the trails of tears and mucus on the baby's face.

She picks up the child and carries her back to the bedroom, gets under the sheet and lies next to her. 'Stop crying,' she says quietly, looking at the ceiling. 'Everything's okay. You're in my bed. You have what you want.' She laughs a strange, harsh laugh. 'You have what you want,' she repeats, this time to herself. Her forehead burns hot, and small needles of pain threaten the back of her throat, yet there is a release from the leaden exhaustion of the last few weeks, or perhaps it is months now. The baby is still crying, but the sound registers with her only as fact.

She will have to stop the baby crying. She puts on the white nightdress that is tangled in the sheet, and carries her downstairs. She has the odd sensation that she is watching herself as she moves about the kitchen, opening the French doors to the garden, taking the lid off the can of formula. David would normally have prepared the bottles before they went to bed. He would have got up to do a feed, but he has been away the last three nights. He will have told her which town, which hotel, who else will be there from his department; all details of no consequence. He will return tomorrow night, a point that is so far away in her own version of time, it may as well be next week.

Her heart beats faster than usual as she measures out the formula, and her nightdress sticks damply to her back. She stands by the high chair, supporting the bottle in the baby's mouth with one hand as she stares through the open doors into the garden.

The lawn has been draped in silver by the moonlight, offering the promise of coolness under her hot feet. When the baby has emptied and dropped the bottle onto the floor, she hesitates for a moment looking at the last drops of milk spilling onto the dark wood, and glides with her through the doors. She perches her on her hip and the baby, drowsy now she is full, grasps a handful of the white cotton nightdress as her mother bends to breathe in the scent of the neglected roses hanging heavy on their bolting stems. Underneath, the ground is strewn with petals that have given away their delicate pink blush to shine pale and colourless under the moon.

Away from the thick heat inside the house, she whirls slowly around the garden, her face turned up to the sky. The moon is almost full, and she picks out the geography of imagined oceans and continents, feels lightheaded at her smallness, at the insignificance of the two of them beneath the stars.

When she looks down, the baby is asleep, and her first thought is to return to bed, but sleep has lost its allure now. The kitchen spills its harsh yellow light onto the patio, and she can see the unwashed dishes piled, unscraped, along the worktop. The buggy is just inside the doors and she pulls it out, reclines the back and lowers the baby in, draping the pram blanket loosely over her. She bumps it gently down the step onto the grass, and crosses the lawn to the back gate.

Her nightdress catches on the gatepost as they go through, ripping as she pulls it free. The path that runs along the back of the row of gardens is baked hard and flat, and the buggy's tyres turn silently over it. At the end of the path she turns on to another that leads down to the river, and the ground becomes softer, giving slightly under her feet so that she can feel each of her toes pressing into the ground, every blade of grass, every stalk, every stone. The burning heat of a nettle sting blooms on her ankle but she takes pleasure in the quick pain of it, and pushes on, a film of sweat pricking at her hairline and under her arms, the nightdress swishing softly about her knees.

The footpath leads down to a pasture where cattle graze in summer. She and David picnicked here last summer just after they moved to the village, the baby forming inside her. David had packed lemon wedges to squeeze over the smoked salmon, a half–size bottle of champagne that she had guiltily shared. He had rested his head on her lap while she fed him strawberries, watching families with their children kicking balls, messing about with rubber dinghies on the water. They had sighed and said that this was the life. But everything looks different now. The world is a negative of itself. The coats of the cows bunched further along the river are black in the moonlight instead of their usual gleaming chestnut brown.

She leaves the buggy a few feet from the riverbank and stands at the edge. For a moment she thinks she hears someone behind her and turns sharply, but it is the sound of her own breath, rapid and shallow. A rope hangs motionless over the water from a branch of the willow on the opposite bank. At the picnic, they had watched boys swinging from it, whooping and yelling before dropping into the water. There was one girl in the group, maybe a younger sister, who scrambled quickly up the tree and along the branch before she could be shoved out of the way. She did not shout or scream when she swung; her expression was serious, as though she was perfecting a gymnastic routine instead of leaping into a river on a hot afternoon.

What had given that girl her quiet determination? She has tried to picture many times what the baby will be like when she grows up, when she is a teenager, when she is seven or eight like the girl dropping silently from the rope, but she cannot. The idea of walking her to school, holding her hand, plaiting her hair in the morning, is as distant as the picnic now feels.

A darting fish causes a ripple to spread over the still surface of the water. She sits and lowers her legs into the slowly moving current underneath. She can feel the dirt from the walk dislodge from between her toes, the hairs on her legs lift in the slight pull of the silky current over her skin. In one swift movement, she pushes down on her hands and lifts herself up and into the water, taking herself by surprise. It is a relief not to be in control of her body, to have it make the decisions for her. The riverbed is soft and sucks at her feet as she shifts her weight to find her balance. She stretches out her arms and the nightdress rises to the surface to form a white circle around her. She draws up her feet, extends them out in front of her and floats on her back, letting the water fill her ears. Weightless, she stares into the sky, beyond the brightest constellations to the smaller ones behind. The longer she looks, the more stars reveal themselves, multiplying endlessly, joining together so that soon there are more stars than sky, and she is no longer in the water, but floating in the sky with the stars.

Her head bumps softly against something and she jerks upright, treading water, searching for the riverbed with one foot, then the other. She has drifted downriver and into the bank. The rushing and gurgling of river water draining from her ears is pierced by a sharper sound, the baby crying further up the river. She can make out the buggy, surrounded by the looming dark shapes of the cows. A surge of cold and fear courses through her. The river is deeper here and she cannot touch the bottom. 'Get away,' she shouts, but her voice is too small so close to the water. She grabs at tufts of grass on the bank, tries to haul herself up. She does not have the strength. One of the cows has stepped forward towards the buggy, its head lowered.

'Lucy!' she screams. She must not scream, she will need every ounce of strength to get out. Further down there is a place where the bank slopes into the water, where she remembers seeing the cows gather to drink. She swims towards it, tries to find a rhythm that she can draw on to control the terror rising in her. The nightdress clings to her legs, slowing her down.

She stumbles and slips as she emerges from the river. She hitches up the nightdress, races across the grass, yelling in a voice she has not heard before. 'Get away, get *away* from her.' Three of the cows have stepped up to the buggy and one noses it curiously. Alarmed by her roaring and screaming, they jostle together. She flaps her arms wildly and as they back off, one of them turns. Its rump catches the buggy - lifts it onto two wheels - while time is stretched out, suspended, until it lands squarely.

She scoops the baby out and holds her close to her chest. 'It's okay, Lucy, hush now, it's alright, I'm back. We're okay,' and she rocks her, gasping into her hair, wrapping her tightly in the blanket. She walks her round and round in jagged circles with her cheek pressed up against her own, until she is quiet.

The cows have retreated along the riverbank and are grazing quietly as if nothing has happened. Her teeth chattering, she lowers Lucy into the buggy and fastens the straps. Her skin is clammy and cold under the stained and sodden nightdress as she heads towards the gate onto the footpath. Shaking now, she blames the fever; she must have been desperate to cool down. She speaks to the sleeping child, telling her what they will do tomorrow, next week, the places she will take her to when she's older, a torrent of plans she is not aware she has made. She does not remember, or else she decides to forget, how she felt when she was in the river, floating with the stars.

Cornflake Girl

- Lora Stimson -

Two hundred and fifty grams of cornflakes hit a table top. It's a pretty sound. A delicate *shhhuuuiiiii*. Here's how I do it; unfold the plastic sheet; lay it across the table; upturn the box; sort through the flakes to eliminate the defective ones; burnt, broken, too light, too dark. I wear surgical gloves. It feels medical, important. I have been doing this for four days, over and over. The shoot couldn't afford a proper food technician so they got me; recent graduate with a film studies degree and Food Technology A-level. The agency told me only three people applied. The agency told me it didn't pay very well. The agency didn't make me feel good about myself. But after too many months back at the family home - daytime television, cheese on toast, duvet - the fee didn't look so bad. My parents had a fight about it. It's too soon, my mother said. She needs to get back to normal, my father said.

> On the day before graduation I rolled my clothes as small
> as they would go and lay them in the bottom of a duffle
> bag. My pint of milk in the fridge was going out of date, so
> I drank it, one hit, straight from the carton.

There are five people on the crew - Adam the Director, a soft voiced, soft bellied man; Lighting Mo, who is constantly plugged in to headphones; Keith the Cameraman, whose shorts reveal calf muscles tight as chicken fillets. We are here to capture the cornflakes at their best. Whilst we attempt this, there is Lloyd to serve us tea. Lloyd is a media studies graduate and is the single most enthusiastic person I have ever met. I am the only girl.

> On the day before graduation I decided I wouldn't need

my laptop anymore. It was old and cranky, with a broken F3 key but in perfect working order. I gave it to the man who sits beside the old Barclays with his ferret, asking for change.

It is Thursday. When I've finished this packet I will have processed eight hundred grams of cornflakes. I have this down to an art. I pour a third onto the sheet. *Shhhuuuiii*. I spread them carefully. I stand back, assess. I identify the outcasts, drop them into the metal wastepaper basket under the table. These are the flakes that will never know fame.

It's an unappetising word, *flake*. It makes me think of dandruff.

I work my way across the table selecting the largest. In this third there are twenty three suitable flakes. To keep them intact I have a second, smaller table, on which I set them in lines. I repeat this three times until the whole packet has been sorted. In the corner Adam the Director is talking quietly with Keith, scribbling across an A4 document. He seems so sure about what he's doing. I can't imagine being that sure about anything. Trying to imagine it gives me a large and uncontainable feeling. It makes me feel sick. Mo is leaning against the coffee station flicking through a magazine, twisting his little finger inside his left ear.

I survey my table of cornflakes, in lines like a cereal army. Lloyd's job is to clear up and bring me a bowl. I set the bowl on digital scales, zero them. Then arrange the cornflakes in the bowl until I have exactly thirty grams. Not twenty nine, not thirty one, Adam said on the first day. A portion of cornflakes is thirty grams. His voice was quiet and careful. We need thirty grams of the best cornflakes. We may need them thirty times over the course of the shoot. Are you okay with that? I noticed that he had long eyelashes and very green eyes. I wondered what he would say had I not been okay with it.

Before today we did three days of close ups. It was my job to pour the milk from a height, so it splashed in a particular way. We used full fat milk watered down 5:1, shaken then left to settle for exactly five minutes. When I asked Adam why we didn't just use semi skimmed he said that semi skimmed and watered down whole milk have a completely different look and viscosity. I tried to ignore the uncontainable feeling.

On the day before graduation I took my books to the
charity shop, deleted my email account and unlaced all my
trainers. Then I threw my bedding into the garden and
set it alight using barbeque firelighters. It took a long time
to flare and an even longer time to burn. It caught the
rosemary bush, which began to sizzle and pop. It smelled
wonderful. Alice came into the garden and screamed at me,
asking what the hell I was doing. She screamed so hard that
it made me cry.

Between takes there is nothing to do. It is eleven fifteen. The first bowl shot
wasn't right, so I have a second army ready, waiting in lines on the table. Adam
wants me to put the flakes in the bowl at the very last moment. I don't question
him. Adam sends Lloyd off to a coffee shop across town with a complicated
drinks order. He does a good job of making us all feel indispensable, no matter
how menial our role. I suspect that the routine for watering down the milk is
an invention to make me feel more useful. Adam goes out for a cigarette and I
follow him, eager for a change of scene. The studio is a huge empty space at the
end of a corridor on the second floor of a factory building that is presumably full
of other huge, empty spaces. We lean against the red brick wall outside. It is a still,
damp day. The sky is purpled, ready to rain but it's not cold and Adam un-buttons
his coat. He starts at the bottom and works his way toward his chin. He has
been wearing the coat all morning and now reveals the black shirt he's wearing
underneath. I like noticing the way people remove their clothes. He offers me a
cigarette and I decline.

On the day before graduation I imagined I was a caterpillar,
I stilled my mind and concentrated on growing a cocoon.
I thought about the butterfly inside. Always the butterfly,
nothing else. I concentrated on not being the caterpillar.

I worked with a raisin girl once, Adam says suddenly. An ad shoot in Argentina.

We had to film raisins. There was nothing else in the shot, just raisins. At least we have milk on this one. I think he is making a joke and go to laugh but, when I turn to him, his face is serious. So, what does a raisin girl do? I ask. The same, he says. Just with raisins. Was she good at it? I ask. I realise this is a stupid thing to say but at the same time I want to know. I have learnt that there is nothing simple about arranging food. I have learnt that this is something Adam takes very seriously. Yes, Adam says. She didn't speak any English though, so it was difficult. But, she was very good. Adam pulls on his cigarette. How is the hotel? he asks. Fine, I say. I tell him about the Greek receptionist who keeps calling me by the wrong name. Adam smiles. It takes me by surprise. It changes his face into something warm and shining. Where are you staying? I ask. Another hotel, he says. In the distance an electronic voice tells us that a vehicle is reversing. Do you always direct food adverts? I ask. Yes, he says. There is a snail crawling up the wall next to him. What do you want to do, after this? he asks. I tell him that I don't know. I don't tell him that I don't want to do anything. That I am trying really hard. That everyone else makes it look so easy. Don't get into this, Adam says, it's boring as shit. I have never heard him swear before. I thought you liked it, I reply, you are so good at it. I feel silly having said it. Lloyd arrives with the coffee; he is practically running across the car park.

> On the day before graduation I swallowed thirty three
> paracetamol tablets with a bottle of white wine and waited.
> In the hospital, when they asked me where I had got the
> tablets I said I had stolen them from my housemates'
> rooms. I did not say I had bought them that day from three
> different chemists. That I had intended on taking all forty
> eight but had suddenly panicked.

Cornflakes are like fallen leaves. At first they are individually beautiful. If you listen closely enough, they each make a unique sound. They each have their own particular shade. If you look at one long enough you could pick it out of a crowd. But given time - and accumulation - they don't just become mundane, they become sickening. And then they are everywhere. Cornflakes clogging the pavement gullies. Cornflakes in the local park, choking up the children's slide. Cornflakes windblown across the foyer. They flutter into your dreams and bury you.

In my hotel room I clean my shoes with a paper towel from the bathroom. I choose my clothes for tomorrow and hang them over the front of the wardrobe door. I start up my laptop - the laptop my father bought me when I went to live back at home. I open a Word document and write the word *flake* in the middle of the page. I think of synonyms and write a list;

cornshaving
cornsliver
cornscale
cornfragment

My room is beside the lift shaft, I can hear it rumbling quietly through the wall, getting incrementally louder as it passes my room and down into the guts of the hotel.

cornshred
cornsplinter
cornportion

Like a snowflake. Each one unique.

I switch on the hotel television. There is an advert for washing powder. I imagine a girl somewhere, sifting crumbs of washing powder with a pair of tweezers. I turn the television off and play some music through my laptop. My mother sends a text to ask how I am, as she does at the end of every day. I wonder how long this will go on for. Someone knocks at the door and when I open it Adam is standing there. I wondered if you wanted a drink, he says. He is holding a bottle of wine. We sit on the end of the queen size bed and Adam pours the wine into hotel coffee cups. I ask him where else he's been on shoots. Frankfurt, Shanghai,

Swansea, he says. Stockholm. Lots of places that start with S. He pauses. Sheffield, I like Sheffield. All hotel rooms look the same though, don't they? I'm not sure if I'm supposed to answer. I haven't even unpacked, I say. We both look at my bag on the suitcase rack. I never unpack, Adam says - I'm hardly ever home. Three bedrooms, he says, I'm never even there; it's ridiculous. I wonder if he has a girlfriend, or a cat. I choose not to ask, preferring to imagine. I imagine him coming home, setting his suitcase down. I imagine him going into his bathroom. Beside the sink, hotel miniatures of shampoo and shower gel are lined up in rows. There is a toothbrush in a glass and a tube of travel toothpaste. I imagine him waking up in the morning and momentarily forgetting which country he is in.

He scrolls through the playlist on my computer. Would you prefer to go out? I ask. You must be sick of hotel rooms. No, he says. I'm happy here. I have the urge to kiss him and so I do. We stop kissing and I look at him, trying to gauge how old he is, thirty nine, forty, perhaps older. There is something incredibly wrong about kissing him and it makes me want to do it more. We are setting our coffee cups on the floor, laying ourselves across the bed. I wonder if this is what he came here for. I move my hand underneath his shirt, his skin is soft. The bulge of his belly presses against me.

Hotel sheets pulled across us I ask Adam what will happen tomorrow. More close ups, he says. But that's not what I mean. I don't think I'll ever be able to look at another cornflake again, I say. I feel the same way about raisins, he says quietly, to himself. They're not for me, I think - these cornflakes and film sets and lighting rigs. But there are other things. In the quiet, thoughts of other things fill me.

Soon, I will ask Adam to leave. I will lie in the dark, waiting. Listening to the lift rumble through the wall, listening to my own breath. Up and down, up and down.

Mount Sanitas

- Melissa Fu -

The mountain wakes me before dawn. Its call cuts through a fog of restlessness that has clouded the night. I shrug off the blankets and touch my bare feet to the wooden floorboards. Pulling on jeans and a sweatshirt, I head over to the window. The street is quiet, no cars rumble by. To the west stands Mount Sanitas. As I raise my eyes to its silhouette under the stars, I'm filled with a longing to walk its trails, pass into its dimensions.

I ride my bike up Mapleton Avenue, through pools of light from streetlamps, past darkened windows of stately homes with grand porches. It is the season when early mornings hover just above freezing and leaves flash hints of amber and crimson from their edges. My nose and fingers are numb, but warmth builds in my muscles as I cycle beyond the last of the houses to the deserted, dirt-surfaced parking area. Leaving my bike behind, I approach the trailhead.

I start to climb the west ridge trail which snakes through a valley between Mount Sanitas and higher ranges further west. The foothills are filled with crevices like this, rough passageways that lead to peaks overlooking Boulder. In the dimness, everything is muted. Colours are washed over in dawn greys and shades of brown. Even the air feels slower, quieter. The dusty incline is managed by steps made of split logs meant to prevent too many footprints from eroding the soft, rusty soil. I relish how the pull in my quads makes me aware of the effort needed to ascend. When the slope lessens, I pause near a grove of piñon trees and pick up fallen cones, twisting their rough scales to look for any nuts left behind by squirrels. I scavenge a few small brown kernels and pocket them for later, hoping to find sweet nutmeats inside the hard shells.

With a sudden certainty, I know I want to reach the mountain's summit before the sun spills light over the horizon. Birdsong prompts me to hurry.

Leaving the piñons and pushing the pace a little, I continue along a footpath that weaves through a cluster of scrub oak. Heart beating fast in my chest and thumping in my ears, I am greedy for morning mountain air.

This is never a lonely place, but it is a hike I always take alone. I have walked other, longer trails in the company of friends, rambling in the Rockies for miles. But the west ridge of Mount Sanitas, though steep and rugged, is a short route, rising 1300 feet in just over a mile. This mountain summons when I most need perspective; instinct delivers me here again and again. Yet its paths never fail to fool me. They tease with false summits, with peek-a-boo finality. Whenever I think I must be near the peak, an unexpected turn reveals another ascent. The route zig-zags and disappears around blind-corners, presenting me with challenging rocks. I take a spur off the main path to the edge of the ridge and gaze on the valley below, a sense of accomplishment arising from the heights I have climbed. Turning my head, I see how far I still have to go.

As I follow the trail, I fall into a rhythm of walking and breathing. The movement disperses any threads of complicated thought, my mind mesmerised instead by the pendulum swing of arms and legs. No inner chill remains. I stride through a stand of pines, climb another group of boulders, and, startled, find myself at the top. However many times I've walked this path, the true summit is always a surprise. The mountain cradles me with the Rockies at my back and Boulder at my feet.

I am looking down on a child's toy town built with coloured wooden blocks and matchbox cars. The parking lots are empty, the traffic signals a long sequence of green lights. The grid of the city stretches out way beyond, interrupted by the irregular shape of the reservoir, and further east I see open space, nothing but plains and prairie, stretching past imaginary state lines.

Sitting on the crest, waiting for the sun, my pulse slows and breath deepens. I rub my sticky thumb and index finger together and inhale the scent of piñon sap. Not a nerve, not a muscle in me wants to move. I sink into the mountain's presence, its solemn indifference to the dramas that play out at its feet, its patient fortitude through wind, rain, snow. Reaching the top is not a victory; it is a homecoming.

Just as the chill begins to penetrate my stillness, when the sweat from my earlier exertion is turning into cold droplets down my back, when goosebumps are rising on my arms, the horizon breaks with brightness. Rays come racing across the eastern plains, rising up to meet my face, warming my cheeks, painting the rocks on the mountainside, casting sharp shadows westward. I am drenched in radiance. Replete with sun. I stand, eyes closed, shoulders back, palms open, gathering armfuls of light.

The Oversight

- Abby Erwin -

17 February 2013

The crooked peal of sirens and his cheek against the unHoovered floor. He hears them let themselves in and in his mind they are burglars but he is too tired to be afraid. The weave of the carpet has pressed into his cheek and laid a new pattern over the wrinkles already there. The lights have been on all night.

Their voices are far away, then near, and say things like 'You're ok,' and 'It's going to be alright,' and he wonders how they can be so certain. The mouth of the ambulance yawns wide and they slide him neatly into it. He wants to ask how long he'll be gone, whether someone will feed the cat, but his face feels like it's been draped with heavy rubber and he can't make the words.

20 February 2013

The nurse sings, 'You're still young, that's your fault, there's so much you have to know,' and it's the first thing he hears when he wakes up. He thinks she's singing to him but she's doing something with the needle and the tube in his arm and she's singing to the fat clear bag of glucose on the stand.

'Where am I?' he asks, because he feels like he ought to, even though he's pretty sure he knows. They've taken his teeth out; he can see them in a glass on the table next to his bed but he doesn't have the strength to reach for them.

'St Mary's, love,' she says. As she speaks he realises he's peeing and he wants to apologise but he's too ashamed to tell her. He waits for the wet warm feeling followed by the cold and the stickiness that he remembers from childhood but it doesn't come.

The nurse smiles at him. 'Catheter,' she says, as though reading his mind. The word crawls around his brain like an insect before he can assemble it into meaning.

He listens to her move on to the next bed, still singing, 'Find a girl, settle down, if you want you can marry.' The spaces in his head fill with cotton wool and he drifts away again.

15 March 2013

'The Ides of March!' says the social worker as she writes the date at the top of her report. She smiles and he decides it's meant to be a joke.

He's sitting up in bed, still in his hospital gown but with a clean jumper over the top that someone, he doesn't know who, fetched from his house. The sleeve of the social worker's cardigan is unraveling at the cuff; the threads are hanging down and she keeps pushing them aside as she writes.

He remembers his mum knitting when she was alive, making tiny squares and hexagons and stitching them together into mosaicked blankets. He still has one, in a chest or a cardboard box in the loft. He hasn't been up there for years. When he gets home, he'll find it and put it on the sofa. They'll have to let him out soon.

'Is there anyone who can help you at home?' the social worker asks.

He shakes his head. He knows it's not the right answer.

She bites the end of her pen and frowns and writes it down.

22 March 2013

There's a smell of fish in the corridor outside his room. When the girl comes with his pills he mentions it.

'We always have fish on Fridays,' she says. 'You'll get used to it.'

He listens to her feet lino-squeak across the floor. 'I'm only here for a little while,' he says. 'I'll be home soon.'

She smiles and checks his mouth to make sure the pills have gone down.

The social worker told him he had to go somewhere where he could be looked after for a bit, until he was well enough to go home. It's better than the hospital; he has his own room now, with a bed and a chair and a window hung with beige curtains. He has a calendar next to his bed where he marks off the days with a stump of pencil. Sometimes he forgets and then he has to do two the next day and hope that it's right.

He asks if someone can get him the blanket from his house and the girl says she'll do her best, but when she asks where it is he can't remember if it's in the loft or under the bed or if he threw it away years ago. So instead he asks her when he's going home, but she doesn't know, nobody's told her.

15 April 2013

The girl's name is Elena and she has dark eyebrows and lashes like a girl he took to a dance once years ago. He says her name a lot so that he remembers it, 'Elena Elena Elena,' every day when she comes with his breakfast. She shows her crooked teeth and pink gums when she laughs.

'I like your dress,' he says, and she raises the hem of her green uniform and curtseys.

Every day he eats and he takes his pills and then he goes to the lounge and waits for the social worker to return and tell him he's going home.

'Your lady friend?' Elena says and she winks. He asks her if he can make a call and she brings him the phone, but the social worker never gave him a number and he can't remember what her name was. Elena asks him if there's anyone else he wants to call but the only names he can think of are the names of the dead.

2 June 2013

His room is a sticky dense cube of heat like Turkish Delight. All the residents are given whirring electric fans that do nothing but cut the air into smaller pieces.

Elena closes the heavy curtains and refills the plastic jug of water next to his bed. When she leaves he rises slowly with his joints clicking and opens the curtains again so he can watch the summer twilight over the parking lot and the roofs of the semis outside. The water he drinks obediently.

At home he sat up late watching television and often woke in the morning to the chattering voices of the breakfast show, still in his chair. Here he is put to bed like a child and lies awake for hours, listening to cries and fits of coughing through the walls.

Eventually he sleeps. He dreams that his house is full of children but their faces are old, older even than his, and they reach out to him with their withered hands. They clutch at the bottom of his trousers and he kicks them away and they scurry from him and wrap their faces in the apron of a towering mother.

When he wakes his sheets are sticking to his legs with sweat. Then he realises it isn't sweat. He strips the sheets from the bed and looks around for somewhere to hide them – the wardrobe? The narrow chest of drawers? He goes to the window to drop them out but when he gets there he remembers it doesn't open.

23 July 2013

He eats his lunch in a room full of nodding heads. Hot and still and it smells like sprouts.

In the evening Elena tells him that the new baby prince has been born.

'I love your Royal Family,' she says. 'I have a scrapbook where I put newspaper clippings, things like that. I'll show you if you like.'

'Do you have any children?' he asks her.

She looks out the window. 'One day. Do you?'

'No,' he says. 'Never married.'

She waits as he swallows his pills. 'You never know.' She winks at him over her shoulder on her way out the door.

10 September 2013

A river runs through the radiator next to his bed. The days are getting shorter and he responds by waking earlier as though to claw them back.

He stops sitting in the lounge during the day, keeping to his room instead. He sits with his back to the window. He isn't sure what he's waiting for.

When the girl comes with his pills it isn't Elena. Her face is unfamiliar and she has a tattoo of a butterfly crawling up her neck over the collar of her uniform. She says, 'Good morning,' but she doesn't ask how he is and he's still not dressed so she starts trying to unbutton his pajama jacket.

'No!' He pushes her hands away. It comes out louder than he meant it and the girl jumps back from him like he's hit her.

Elena comes to see him in the evening even though he's not on her rounds and he grabs hold of her hand and won't let go. He can tell he's squeezing too hard and hurting her but she doesn't say anything. She sits next to him on the bed and tears run down his face and fill his mouth with salt.

1 November 2013

He lies in bed all day watching a spider move up the wall. It disappears behind the curtain and he cries. He thinks of his cat and he cries. He remembers staying home from school with a fever when he was a little boy and staring all day at the pattern on the wallpaper until it became more real to him than the world outside.

Elena brings him a poppy from the supermarket. She leaves it on the bedside table next to the calendar.

'The doctor will come tomorrow,' she says. 'If you don't get up soon, get dressed, eat something, they'll send you back to the hospital.'

When she returns that evening he's sitting in his chair by the window, the poppy pinned neatly to his lapel.

27 December 2013

Many of the residents have been taken home for Christmas, collected by sons and nieces and brothers and granddaughters. The lounge is empty so he sits there, half-reading old copies of *Yours,* and sleeping, and watching the paperchains that criss-cross the ceiling slowly droop from their moorings as the blu-tack loses its hold.

'Will you go back home, for Christmas?' he asked Elena at the beginning of the month but she shook her head and said she couldn't afford it and privately he was relieved.

She sits with him in the afternoon when she has a free quarter hour and they play cards but there's too many missing from the pack. Instead he starts to tell her about Christmas during the war, how he and his brother caught a rabbit for dinner and his mother made the pudding out of carrots and breadcrumbs.

'You've told me that one before,' Elena says and squeezes his hand and then she has to go back to work.

15 January 2014

Rain shivers against his window. He keeps forgetting to ask Elena for a new calendar and there's a dustless rectangle on his bedside table where the old one used to be. He tries to remember the last time he was cold, or wet, or hungry. His skin feels dull and lacquered, his lips flaky with dry skin from the central heating.

There's a knock on his door. It's the girl with the butterfly. 'Someone's here to see you,' she says, and she takes him to the manager's office.

The manager's mouth is a hard flat line. There's a young, plump woman sitting on the other side of her desk.

'Hi,' she says. 'I'm Megan. I'm a social worker. We're going to try and get you home.'

He sits on a hard plastic chair and drinks weak coffee.

'I can only apologise,' Megan says. 'There was an error in the system, a simple oversight… My colleague went on sick leave, we misplaced her notes.'

'Did you forget about me?' he asks.

Megan's face is pink. 'Unfortunately these things happen sometimes. Now that we're aware of the situation, we're going to try and get your case sorted as quickly as possible.'

'Am I going home then?'

He thinks of his empty house, frozen sepia in time, and a wave of nausea passes over him.

2 February 2014

Elena strips the bed for the last time and he watches her do it. He wants to give her something, flowers or chocolates or an envelope of cash, but he hasn't had money for months. He wishes he could take a step towards her and embrace her or just lay a hand on her cheek but Megan is waiting for him in the corridor. His things have already been packed and taken away.

Elena turns to him with the bundled sheets in her arms and she smiles and it's like a pane of glass has been laid over her face. 'Good luck,' she says, and she transfers the sheets to her trolley and shakes his hand. 'We'll miss you.'

She leans in and does up the top button of his jacket and she moves on to the next room as he takes his first steps down the corridor towards the cold and waiting world.

The Outside Woman

- Tricia Abraham -

Arlene Brathwaite fans sheself with impatience, stamping she right foot and sucking she teet in frustration. The public bus has broken down again. The driver pointing to de door with his thumb saying, 'Ged out.'

Off-loading onto the side of de road, Arlene moves to the shade of a tamarind tree, blowing out de red dust flying into she nostrils from passing traffic. She nods she head in agreement when a dark skinny girl says to no one in particular, 'Comin down dem mountain roads does always upset de brakes. Dey does start smelling stink, like castor oil and cane fyah burning all at once.'

Private taxis are quick to pick up de younger, more aggressive passengers. But Arlene has no intention of putting she life at risk, those madmen drive around corners on two wheels, blasting dub music, the beat vibrating de surrounding air.

One funeral for the day is enuff.

Another bus pulls up twenty minutes later, and all she can do is hold onta she hat and handbag whilst being swept up wid de crowd pushing fuh de door. She finds a seat and begins ta fix sheself. Patsie has done a good job wid de black dress, it is not too tight, with a square neck and empire waist ta give she room to move. A little too short in de hem, but no matter, she is wearing she muddah's heavy stockings to cover up she bare legs and she black patent church shoes. She has the matching bag, it looks too dressy wid de sequin and diamante pattern, but de broad-rimmed Panama hat balances out everything against she light brown complexion. She wears the pearl choker Oscar gave her last Christmas. Lord, how she hounded him fuh it.

Arlene is a handsome woman, high cheekbones, broad flat nose, and thick full lips. But she inherit she muddah's eyes, weighted underneath with half-moon folds of skin pulling down at de corners. She muddah say dat each line represent every trouble dat Arlene ever cause. Arlene ain't sure whose eyes she muddah talking bout, she own, Arlene's or both. Arlene pats she sweaty brow with a small towel thinking, ah had ta get de last seat right in de hot sun, and ta top it off, dis pock-face, fat lip man next to me only trying to feel muh up. Arlene bends over to dab the towel behind she hot knees, sweat leaving a wet stain on she stockings. Straightening up, she notices de man checking out she backside and breasts.

She noticed right from de start dat Oscar was a breast man. They met in de rum shop where she cooked fishcakes on Friday nights. He ordered a double portion with plenty pepper sauce. Bending low over the bar ta eat them right in line with she breasts, grease dribbling down de side of he mout, a heavy sweat shining he forehead. They chatted until all de batter was finished. Then he walked her home, leaning into she neck blowing his oily breath into her ear, singing the tune, 'There's a brown gal in the ring, tra, la, la, la, la… show me a motion,' squeezing she breast. Arlene had broken away with a loud giggle, signalling a sharp, scolding cough from she muddah inside the house. Arlene's muddah warn she bout Oscar, 'You watch it gal, de same mout that court you, don't marry you.'

Two months lata he had set Arlene up in a small house near de rum shop. Next ting she know she was 'pushing breadcart', she pregnant belly straining against she clothes. How tings change so fast? When Arlene went ta tell she muddah, she find she sitting pun de front step shelling peas, she fingers black, her head hanging low. She didn't even look up, but Arlene could see de tears dropping into de bowl. She muddah tell she, 'Iz what more shame you could bring on our name, gal?' Arlene feel sorry for she muddah, is not like she had an easy life. When de news spread round de village, Arlene was only four years old, so people wasn't unkind to she, but dey was mean ta she muddah. Like is she fault she husband had an affair wid de vicar wife. Like only if she was a good enuff woman, he woulda stay at home and be happy wid only she.

'I neva thought I could eva feel dis same pain and shame again, like I feel when you faddah left me. I have tried my best. But Arlene, you seem bent on walking a path that I cannot walk wid you. I always tell you, neva draw yuh chair where yuh table ain't lay.' There was a moment of silence, and then she muddah shoulders drop as if two concrete slabs just slip off. She muddah let out a big sigh, saying, 'You gots ta go now Arlene.'

Arlene was trembling, 'But Ma…'

'Go.'

She muddah neva look up from de bowl of peas, and she neva look Arlene in de eye again.

Oscar demanded she cook fishcakes every day. Whilst in front of de stove, he liked ta grab Arlene from behind, his two hands wrap under she heavy tits, as if weighing up two pumpkins in de market, he hips grinding into she round bottom, moaning with pleasure. Oscar used ta say dat he like a little meat pun he bones. Dat it mek the eating all de more sweeter and juicy. Lord, dat man had a dirty tongue! Arlene chuckles out loud at de memory.

The pock-face man notices his opening and wastes no time, a slick sideways grin on he face, toothpick rolling between he teet.

'Buoy you smell sweet fuh days. Iz where you goin lookin so fine?'

Arlene squints she eyes at him in disgust, pouting she lips. She turns ta de window, giving him a dismissive suck of she teeth. Where indeed? Why dat man Oscar just had ta up and die? Where dat goin leave she? How she goin put food pun de table when she can barely afford dis trip down inta town? Arlene sucks she teet in anger. The fat-lip man thinks it's fuh he, and snatches his hand away from next to she thigh.

Arlene told Oscar he can't only eat pork chops and fishcakes all day. Dem people on de radio had said dat food from de old times had plenty vitamins, all de ground provisions and root vegetables from dem slave days; yams, eddoes, sweet potato. Arlene thought de reference to 'slave days' might trigger a change in Oscar's diet. He like ta talk politicks wid de boys, or as he called it, 'poli-tricks!' Saying how we black people should tek back what iz ours. Dat plantation days done! Dat we need ta get back ta our roots. He even order some Kente cloth from de back of Boysie's van, saying how he honouring he Ashanti ancestors. Never mind when he walk in dem rum shop with just de cloth tie round he waist, and a piece drape over he left shoulder. Teets and Tall Boy fall off dem chair laughing, saying how he look like some tourist pun de beach, wid girlie sarong wrap round he waist. Dat all he missin wuz ta get he hair braid wid beads!

That night Arlene could hear Oscar stomping in de yard, ripping at he skin, naked by de gate, throwing de cloth in de hedge and calling she name so rough, like is she fault he dress up like a fool. Even the dogs knew better than to greet him.

So when Arlene put the plate of boiled yam and sweet potato in front of he, she didn't know what ta expect. But he just screw up he face, pushing de plate away cussing, 'Wha iz dis shite woman? Look, give dis to dem mangey pitbulls in de yard, and fry-up some of dat 'Spam' Harry bring from Brooklyn.'

The announcement in de paper was brief. 'Oscar Theopholus Alleyne: Died 3rd September. Fifty-four years old. Heart Attack. Leaves behind a loving family. Services at St. Mary's Church, 8th September. 3pm. No flowers. Drinks at Ronnie's Bar from 4pm.'

Oscar woulda like dat de service only lasting an hour. He neva like too much 'seriousness' as he would call it. When Arlene was in a mood he would open de windows and shout, 'Leh we get dis seriousness out of de house!' Dis little ritual always broke de mood and made Arlene smile. He would pick up Olive and spin she bout, laughing so hard dey couldn't catch breath. He pretended they were big fans, blowing all de 'seriousness' out of de house.

Olive is just like Oscar, full of back chat and brassy boldness. Arlene always arguing wid she saying, 'You just like you faddah, stubborn fuh days and always wanting ta be wrong and strong. Wrong and strong!' But at night, Olive only want to curl up like a baby in de curve of Arlene's neck, taking deep breaths absorbing her 'muddah smell'. Oscar had de same ritual when he went ta sleep. Even when Arlene's shoulder would turn to pins and needles, and her neck would stiffen, she neva liked ta move him. She happy to feel he legs wrap up tight wid hers, his arm stretch out across she belly, he other hand tucked under her hip. The heavy breath of his snoring fanning out across de bare skin between she breasts. She like to feel the full weight of his sleeping body pun she, like he surrender ta she, like he feel safe next ta she, and, for dat moment, Arlene feel like he really belong ta only she.

Just de memory of dis moment and de realisation dat Oscar really gone start Arlene heart pounding like it goin burst through and jump out she chest, and de tears start ta flow. De man next ta she get up quick and move away. Oscar really gone. And she neva goin feel he body like dat again. And Arlene sheself feel like she dying. Meaning she hear dat people does have dem whole life flash in front of dem de minute before dey die. And dat is what Arlene going through now. She feeling Oscar tickling she neck with he hair, and feeling the breath of Olive in she ear saying, 'But Ma.' And Arlene see she muddah, and dis time she look up from shelling peas and say, 'I goin be wid you gal, whatever comes.'

Arlene know that she muddah would never say dat, but she see it flash in front of she anyway. Den Arlene realise dat she ain't dying, she just talking ta sheself. And she catch she breath and she heart begin ta settle. Arlene decide then and there that she will tek de job that she muddah organised fuh she cleaning Mrs. Clarke's big concrete house six days a week. Mrs. Clarke say if she cleans as well as she muddah, then there will be no problems. Dat one hurt. Is not like Arlene end up right back where she start, but worse, she back to where she muddah start!

Arlene pulls out a small compact and tries ta fix she face, dabbing powder on she oily nose, smoothing over the channels of her tears. The bus stops outside de church. Only thirty minutes late. Thank God, she can still see cars arriving, the coffin sitting in de hearse, back doors open to let de breeze in. Arlene thinks to sheself, I can do this, I ain't got nuthin to be shame bout. I got de right ta be here.

Arlene moves forward to pay she respects to Oscar's wife and children.

The Siren

- Patricia Mullin -

We met digging in the sand. At first my brother and I kept our distance, wary and territorial, afraid that these other children would invade the hole we had dug, knock down our sandcastle, or worse, build a better one. Then a ball strayed and a cautious exchange took place. The boy became excited; I noticed that he kept slipping into a foreign language. He told us that when the tide turned the sea would flow on to our end of the beach and he said we could build a dam and dig a swimming pool; he invited us to join in. We looked at our parents expectantly. Was it safe? my mother enquired. Entirely, their father reassured her, only the far side of the channel was dangerous. The boy butted in, he explained that a siren would sound when the tide turned and you must walk back at once or risk being cut off. He said people had drowned attempting to cross the channel. He enacted a dramatic watery death struggling and gurgling, finally falling silent and limp on the sand. He didn't remain a corpse for long bouncing back up so that names could be exchanged. He must have enjoyed his performance as he re–enacted it year after year for all new holidaymakers.

Their mother, Serefina, was Italian and as she removed her sunglasses I saw that she and her son, Guido, shared the same dark penetrating eyes. The girl, Evie, took after her English father, James. To me, Serefina looked like a film star; her swimming costume was stylish, her hair black and she was shapely with olive skin. I compared her to my own mother whose pale thighs were covered in fine blue lines like the tributaries of a complex river system. My mother spent her days teaching unruly inner–city children and her evenings with a pile of books to mark; I thought it unlikely that Mrs Hillier worked. Our names, Mark and Susan, were dull in comparison, and we were always closely supervised by our mother. I could see that my parents were smitten by this glamorous, carefree family transplanted onto our beach.

We set off, our spades dragging in the sand leaving a meandering trail, suddenly Guido handed me his spade and said,

'I forgot to kiss Mother goodbye.'

He ran back across the beach. I watched as his mother, who by now was reclining on a sun lounger, proffered her cheek. Having delivered his kiss Guido sped towards me and seized the spade from my hand.

'Do you always kiss your mother goodbye?' I asked.

'Of course. I never know when I might see her again.' His unflinching gaze met mine.

'I thought this wasn't dangerous?'

'It isn't, unless I want it to be,' he replied.

He struck out across the beach waving his spade and parrying like a musketeer, periodically flicking his head to remove a stray lock of dark hair from his eyes. He was lithe, agile and long limbed. I guessed that he was older than me.

Guido marked out the rectangle and instructed us to start digging. Mark and I piled sand in a line. Evie worked at a slower pace and said little. Every so often Guido would shout out orders: higher, pack it tighter, dig deeper. We followed his instructions without question. Other children joined in and Guido divided them into work gangs with specific tasks. It was hard as the deeper sand was wet and heavy. An hour later we had cut a rectangle for the swimming pool with a bank of sand forming a levee around it and a gulley cut to channel the water into it. We stood back and waited. At first the water was a gentle trickle with a dirty froth on the forward tide, then it gathered speed. I dipped my feet in.

'Wait!' Guido cried. 'You *must* wait until *I* give the command.'

He stood in the centre of the pool, our imperious master, holding his spade out to repel any overexcited child. Finally, when the water reached the bottom of his swimming trunks, he shouted:

'Now!'

Whooping laughing children leapt into the shallow pool. Mark went ahead of me. I stepped into the water; it was just deep enough to swim; Evie joined me. By now all the children were, splashing or swimming.

'This is a brilliant,' I said.

'It won't last,' Evie responded, 'it never does.' Then she swam to the opposite side and rested in the water impassive and watchful.

I swam and then floated; it was lovely, so much better than waiting for my parents to escort me to the sea and keep watch. Suddenly there was a collective groan. I looked round to see that Guido had breached the retaining sandbank; soon we were all left standing on damp sand. All that digging and building, and Guido had broken it. I looked questioningly at Evie who shrugged her shoulders, climbed out and set off back towards the hut.

'Did you have a lovely time?' Serefina was wearing a kaftan, a wide–brimmed hat and sipping wine.

'Guido broke the dam again,' Evie complained. The resigned inevitability in her tone of voice suggested she expected no sanction or criticism of her brother. I began to understand Evie's brooding, reticent nature.

Summers with the Hilliers continued in much the same vein for the next few years. Our holidays were arranged to coincide. It suited the parents to believe that we children got on, giving them the freedom to sit on the beach sharing wine and enjoying adult conversation without interruption.

Mr Hillier was in the City and only ever came for one week. They had other holidays, their proper holidays as Serefina called them. Coming to the seaside for the Hilliers was for the benefit of their children; fresh air and the advantages of mixing with ordinary, English children. 'They have to understand that not everyone turns left when they enter an aircraft.' I didn't understand the remark until my father explained that for First Class seats one turned to the left. We always turned right. They went skiing and showed us photographs of Guido and Evie haring skilfully down slopes. One year they asked us to join them, but when my father looked into the cost the plan was dropped.

Gradually Evie and I became closer and Mark seemed to get along with Guido who remained in charge and displayed the easy arrogance of the privileged — poor Evie was always in his shadow and inconsequential just for being a girl. Only once did I see her lose her temper with her brother, kicking sand at him in tearful anger and storming off. I went after her and complained about boys in general in an attempt to make her feel better.

Then one year they didn't come and that was the end of our holidays with the Hilliers. My father took the telephone call, Evie had glandular fever and so they'd decided against the English seaside. By now we were teenagers who were beginning to grate on one another and Guido, who was allowed alcohol, proved predictably unpleasant when drunk. One day, on the hut veranda, he made a grab for my breasts and when I pushed him backwards down the steps and onto the sand, his mother just laughed.

'Oh my poor darling — spurned,' she said, and then turning to me. 'Well done Susan. This is all good practice for fending off troublesome boys; you will thank us one day.'

Our parents missed Serefina and James, their absence opened up the yawning conversational gap that middle–aged couples encounter. Mark and I read our books and tried to play beach cricket with a much reduced team. The year after that we holidayed in Corsica instead, and then I went to university to read English. Our parents continued their coastal holidays, occasionally Mark and I would join them for a few days.

The job prospects for a graduate of English were poor. Study something that leads to a decent job, my father suggested. A member of parliament and his vengeful wife had just been jailed for perjury. I was fascinated by the case, the legal process, and the way the egotistical seed of their downfall sheltered inside both of them. I decided to take a law conversion. There was no funding and the fees were a fortune; it meant living in London too. Studying over two years was my only option and I got a part–time job in the stationary department of a luxury store. It sold outrageously priced diaries and journals, hand–bound in the finest leathers and secured with ornate clasps. The cost of the merchandise was such that there was no question of wasting my paltry wages, even on the smallest journal.

One day, as I arranged a display, a group of young people were queuing at the till. Glittering young people with tanned skin dressed casually in artful designer clothes, I was used to the type, trust–fund brats, there were several at law school; I went to serve them. There in front of me was Guido, a beautiful cliché, very tall, dark and exceptionally handsome.

'Guido!'

He looked at me, puzzled.

'Susan,' I reminded him. 'Summer holidays? All that digging in the sand with my brother Mark.' Guido looked uncomfortable. Clearly he did not wish to be publicly reminded of holidaying in Norfolk however trendy it had become.

'Uh, Susan…yes,' he said disdainfully. The friends, two leggy blonds and a hooray–Henry sort of chap that I recognised from a reality television show, listened to our conversation.

'How are your family? Is Evie in London? It would be great to catch up with her,' I said, while wrapping his purchases.

'My parents are very well, thank you — Evie lives in Rome.'

I dealt with the transaction, handed Guido his packages and said goodbye. He was polite but cool. Returning to the display I watched as the group paused beside the monogrammed stationary.

'Who on earth was *that*?' one of the girls asked giggling.

Before Guido could reply the toff goaded him.

'Buckets and spades…doesn't sound your sort of thing Guido.'

'She's a nobody,' Guido said. And then when pushed repeated: 'Really she's *no one*,' he stated emphatically, but they pressed him for more information. 'Mother briefly entertained the absurd idea that we should mix with ordinary children.'

Then they all burst out laughing.

At the beach, I was met by the same breath–taking view; the pale sand stretching effortlessly to greet the horizon, the sea having distanced itself from the shore by several miles. The dunes were dotted with marram grass and holidaymakers basking like indolent seals. In the far distance a heat haze lingered. I spent the afternoon lying in the sun revising for the next round of exams. Later, it got chilly and so I packed up and walked along the causeway to the town.

Sitting down in a café, I ordered hot chocolate. I flicked through a discarded local newspaper filled with wind farm protests and dull civic events. I turned a page and Guido stared out at me. He stood outside a Coroner's Court next to a middle–aged woman; Mrs Templeton.

The article went on to explain that Mr Guido Hillier had organised a party for friends, they swam out to a sandbank and later became cut off by the incoming tide. Mr Hillier agreed that they had enjoyed some wine with their picnic, but stated that no one in the party would have been over the drink drive limit. He had taken the precaution of checking the time of the incoming tide, but then left his watch in the car. Realising they were cut off they swam back across the channel. Two of the group had got into difficulties and one, Juliet Templeton, a trainee broker, had drowned. Her body washed up three weeks later further down the coast.

Shocked, I read on. Mrs Templeton stated that she didn't want any more young lives blighted by this a tragic accident. When asked by the Coroner, Dr Gray, whether he had heard the siren, Guido Hillier said he had but explained that he didn't know what it meant; he was completely unaware of the danger. The Coroner thanked the witnesses for their frank account of the events and made recommendations about improving the warning signs. He expressed his admiration for the dignified composure of Mrs Templeton and her generosity in encouraging the other young people involved in the tragedy to move forward with their lives.

Once again I peered into Guido's empty soul and recalled our conversation.

'Do you always kiss your mother goodbye?'

'Of course, I never know when I might see her again.'

'I thought this wasn't dangerous?'

'It isn't, unless I want it to be.'

I took out my notebook and wrote down the name of the Coroner and sipping the frothy chocolate I began to feel warm again.

Holding Stones

- Thea Smiley -

The dirty, white line separates the road from the verge. I stay close to the windswept, grey-green grass, treading the edge of the muddy tarmac, steadying myself against the suck and rush of each passing car. I am on the wrong side, but that hawthorn hedge is vicious. It forced me into the on-coming traffic. The cars growl at my heels and I make them wait, their indicators twitching, until the road is clear and they can pull past me, clicking over the cat's eyes.

I know you wouldn't approve. You'd want me to turn round and head back to the village, past the post-box and Eileen at the bus-stop, past the peeling phone-box where 'Coins are Not Accepted'. But I'm not going to.

It's good to be out in the open. The house squashes me, gives me corners. Out here I can breathe and stretch and think clearly. In the fields the earth has been turned so completely that it appears to be in motion, choppy and churning like the ocean before a storm. A tractor is at work in the next field and, beyond, lies a farm where small wind turbines spin and a stack of bales collapses in an open-sided barn... The sky is the colour of your favourite shirt, the one with the wine stain on the front. I tried to get that damn stain out, but it wouldn't shift. You didn't care. 'I like it,' you said, and shrugged. 'It makes me look reckless and debauched and authentic: A proper writer.' You admired the stain and smoothed the cotton. The shirt was frayed and faded in places, just like the sky.

The blackberries were sweet this year, and there are still plenty of sloes and rosehips on the hedges near the house. The apple tree produced a good crop, so I made a crumble or two. Oh, and the blue tit is back, pecking at the window putty. I watched it for a while this morning before shooing it away, and it glanced at me like you used to, as you withdrew your hand from the biscuit tin.

I've revived the vegetable patch, harvested the raspberries, and I went to the wood last weekend and kicked the fallen leaves just to acknowledge the season. I saw some tracks - from a deer, perhaps - and, when I stopped to take a closer look, I listened for your footsteps wading through the leaf litter behind me. But all I could hear were pigeons clattering in the tree tops and partridges bowling through the thickets. The breeze made the saplings creak and clack against each other and, beyond the pond, the dark trunks massed and muttered. So I didn't stay long. It's not a place to be alone.

More rubbish in the ditch. Old weather-bleached crisp packets and coke cans, McDonald's cups and plastic bags, even a glass bottle or two. I'd pick them up, but the sides of the ditch are steep and slippery with dead grass and, if I climb in, I may not get out again. Not like you. You clambered in once and cleared it all up, the brambles snagging on your trousers, ditch-water seeping through the seams of your shoes. You shouted: 'Morons!' and grew red in the face. Then you gripped the grass, trusting the pale tufts, as you heaved yourself up, out, and walked on, the filthy haul swinging from your hand. But you were suited to the job. You had a habit of collecting Roman rubbish.

Something is moving among the nettles and the brittle stalks of rosebay willowherb. A rabbit. Its ears are flat, pressed to its back, and its eyes are like a foggy morning.

Walk on, Victoria. Forget it.

We should've done that with the muntjac a few years ago. But you were so thrilled to see it standing beside the hole in the hedge, with its tiny antlers and sleek, brown coat. Only, as we crept closer, we caught a glimpse of the pale silver snare around its neck which tightened each time it leapt. Its eyes flitted from us to the field beyond, and it began to make a harsh, rasping sound. We couldn't calm it down, so hurried home in search of wire cutters and a blanket to hold it still. While I looked in the shed, Mr Johnson leant on the fence and said: 'They're dangerous buggers with a nasty bite.' He told us to leave it alone and phone the farmer.

We made the call. As we walked back down the lane, we heard a gunshot, and the sky was peppered with rooks.

Hold the stones, Victoria. Feel their curves.

Sometimes you said you could smell the sea air blowing in from the east.

It whisked away the stink of silage or muck-spreading from the fields around our house, and sent it to the Saints in the west. The lawless lands, you called them, a place where people got lost for days. A wild area with too many churches and not enough pubs. 'I wouldn't go there,' you told friends with a smile. 'Go north or south if you need me, and you'll find me in the Three Tuns or the Triple Plea.' I knew though that you'd go anywhere with me. We walked the local lanes and footpaths together, places with idyllic names like Hog Lane, Grub Lane, or Deadman's Grave. You sauntered in your old tramp hat - your 'debonair travelling hat'- and stopped every ten paces to pick up a flint, a flower, or a stem of wild grass. It was… frustrating. But I'd be happy to wait for you now.

I went to Walberswick the other day. I found three hag stones, a couple of crab claws, and an old rubber glove which I left on a post to greet the next beach-comber. Then I walked along the shingle bank between the dun-coloured sea and the reed beds and, yes, you were right: the reeds do look like the fur of a hare. It was getting late, so I didn't brave the path and go as far as the old wind pump. Instead, I stared out to sea and imagined you beside me, the stones scuttling and crunching beneath your feet, as you squinted at a distant sail and swore about the power station.

Just after you were made redundant, we walked from the Scallop to the Martello tower and watched the boats on the Alde. Out on that strip of land, with the shallow waves tickling the shingle behind us and the wide river winding towards us, you told me the story about… was it Claudius? You leaned closer. 'In nineteen hundred and seven, a boy was fishing in this river when he felt a weight on his line.'

You paused, delighted to have my attention. I could smell sardines on your breath.

'He tugged and tugged… Reeled in his catch… Hoping that it was an eel… a bass…or even a thresher shark… when up from the depths of the murky river, up to the shimmering surface, rose a head…the head of a Roman emperor, water sloshing in the eye sockets.'

You told me that it was made of bronze, and had been hacked from a statue in Colchester by Boudica's army. For days afterwards the emperor's face kept resurfacing in my mind. It was Boudica who remained in yours, as though after years of teaching the Romans, you had discovered her… or she had come to you, conquered you. Either way, she definitely turned your head.

I never quite understood what she meant to you, despite those nights sitting at the kitchen table, hunched in the circle of light, when you talked about your research and the book you hoped to write. We agreed that she had been mistreated, but we argued too, about her heroism, her rebellion, her place on the curriculum. We turned your treasures in our hands - feathers, pieces of pottery, a weightless, white bird skull - and discussed the Iceni, her tribe, her people. We made plans to visit Snettisham, Thetford, and Caistor St. Edmund. That summer, instead of looking for work, you retreated to the university library and spent afternoons reading and researching, and driving… driving home with a stack of battered books on the passenger seat.

You should've stuck to walking, to wandering and meandering. If all of our walks together had been traced, they would make intricate circles and loose loops through the countryside like the Celtic patterns you admired. So different to this. This Roman road, direct and determined, which runs like a straight, dark line through our lives.

Christ! Car! Too close, too fast. It ripped the air beside me, trailing leaves. The truck was speeding too, the driver on the phone, one hand on the wheel… Tosser.

Last year, the second anniversary, the sky was gloomy and the kitchen like a cave. I turned on all the lights and the radio. As I flicked through the stations, I caught part of an aria, just a few bars, but enough to know what it was, enough to recall the way your voice had croaked and cracked as you'd tried to reach the high notes.

So, I set off despite the rain. Visibility was poor. Windscreens were steamed up and the road was slippery. I kept in, even leapt on the verge at times. The rain thrummed loudly on the flexing umbrella and, when the wind changed, the drops flew horizontally and battered the hood of my coat. Every car that passed dazzled me with its headlights and flicked up a wave of surface water, and the huge, whooshing trucks nearly spun me round. I shouted at them: 'Bastard! Arsehole! Selfish git!' You would've been impressed. But my voice was swept away.

Soon my feet were soaking and my trousers clung coldly to my legs. The rain pummelled the sugar beet in the field, and a gull was blown across the sky. Oak trees writhed as their leaves were torn off, and I had an urge to catch the brown scraps and pin them back on to the branches, to halt autumn, winter, the cold, everything.

In the fields the earth changed to a slick, stubborn clay, and dull water lay in the tractor tracks. The ditch was far from full but the culverts were blocked, choked with leaves and mud and twigs, so the rain could not drain away. Parts of the road flooded, and cars hit the water at speed, the steering wheels wobbling in the drivers' fists. As the water swelled and spilled across the tarmac, I tried to dig a channel with my heel, thumping it into the muddy culvert and dragging it towards the ditch. I tried again and again, scoring my boot across the clogged verge, and still the pool grew. The cars sped past regardless, but at least no one could tell that I was crying.

This year the weather is behaving itself, thank God, although clouds have formed over Bungay, and it looks as though it may be raining in Norwich, the streets glistening beneath the grey sky. City rain makes me think of falling pencils, each drop drawing a line through the air to a dot, like a full stop, on the ground. It seems man-made as though designed to clean the pavements. Here, the unruly rain streams along each piece of grass and slips into the soil, softening the earth and seeking out the seeds of winter wheat, to make them swell and burst like underground fireworks.

A tractor approaches, shaking the sparrows from the hedgerow. The vibrations rise through the soles of my boots and the noise grinds inside me. I keep in, bracing myself as it chunters past flinging mud from its wheels, chased by a rattling trailer. How sleek the tarmac must seem after the rough ground, how small the other vehicles. The driver bounces along in the lofty cab, too young to understand his potential for chaos, so brazen and haphazard.

Hold the stones, Victoria. Rub the sand and earth from their faces.

A kestrel-

-hovering near the field boundary, its wings and tail splayed, its head bowed. It doesn't notice the traffic filing past. It's as focussed as you were at your desk, tapping your pen against your chin, as you read about revolt and massacre. 'Tea?' I asked, breaking Boudica's spell, and you wheeled away from the text like the bird whose prey has escaped. You looked bewildered. Then, gradually, you returned, steadying your descent with your hand on a pile of papers, to find me standing in the doorway in my work clothes. I only realised how many notes you'd made when I tried to tidy your desk last year. Heaps of paper with headings like 'The Conquest' or 'The Aftermath'. I didn't know what to do with it all. I... I considered burning it, scooping it up in my arms and carrying it down to the bottom of the garden, the box of matches rattling in my jacket pocket. But the thought of you sitting, head bowed, stopped me.

So I gave your notes to Robert. He said he would try to finish the work and find a publisher. I didn't want to discuss it. Her.

One night you'd woken so disorientated that you seemed to be spinning, talking of chariot wheels and naked, woad-painted warriors. Another night I had lurched awake to find myself alone, the bed half-cold, while you'd scribbled notes beneath the landing light. Then, there was the morning when the bed shook, and I turned to find you... quietly... laughing. 'I dreamt that I was in the supermarket,' you said, 'and I saw Boudica. She had a tin of ox-tail soup in her basket.'

After that, I didn't want to hear any more. I went out and mowed the lawn, pacing the garden, absorbed in the whir of the machine, the slicing of blades. For a week or two you seemed to return to the present. Some afternoons, you appeared in the shop, admiring the tools, or leaning on my counter and asking where you could find panel pins or decking screws as though you intended to use them. However, on my days off, I would catch you watching me from the kitchen window as I took a rest from gardening or chopping logs, a hoe at my side or an axe in my hand. Then, the distance between us could have been measured in millennia.

I pass the junction and a lane to the Saints. Beside a house, the geese start their reedy honking and run towards the gate, their serrated bills gaping.

Through a fence I glimpse an upturned wheelbarrow- and two pumpkins blazing like planets in a vegetable patch.

One morning, as I was digging up potatoes in our garden, you asked: 'Anything interesting? Any bones?' I shook my head and continued to sift and gather our glowing crop. You stayed where you were, ducking beneath the soft, round leaves of the hazel tree. 'Have you heard of the Sedgeford Hoard?' you said, tugging at the ragged hem of your yellow jumper. I paused and frowned, my foot on the fork. 'Doesn't matter,' you mumbled, and turned towards the house. A worm oozed from between two clods and made its way past my boot. 'Why?' I called, and you… you came back. The washing rippled on the line as you told me that twenty or so Iceni coins had lain hidden in a cow bone for almost two thousand years. I was amazed… not by the facts, but by the look on your face.

The bushes here hold their last few gold leaves or red berries in the air like offerings, and the green corrugated shed guards its patch of hard-standing. Only a few square panes of glass remain in the window frames, and the graffiti says: 'Townies Go Home'.

My pockets are heavy.

I avoided this road for months, drove cross-country, navigating past the gore of roadkill, startling the single magpies along Rumburgh Lane. I went the back way to return your books to the university library. They were late and you received a fine. Those raw days were full of payments and paperwork, of things I had to do, jobs which would've depressed me even if life had been easy, even if you had been with me. I was grateful that the boys came to stay. I gave Robert your yellow jumper and offered Ben your blue shirt, but he didn't want it. So, I wore it myself for a while until your scent faded.

By the first anniversary, the shirt had reached the rag bag in the shed. That morning, the blue tit flew into the kitchen, circumnavigated the doorways, and threw itself at the French windows. It sat stunned on the low sill, its yellow breast puffing. I covered it with a napkin and took it outside. My cupped hands felt empty and, for a moment, I wondered whether the bird was there at all, or had changed into a vapour.

However, back in the house, it had left proof of its presence down the wall. I went to the shed to get a rag and… pulled out your shirt. It smelled musty, so I shook it, holding it up by the shoulders, making the frayed cuffs swing. And, briefly, I saw your shape, your chest, the slope of your stomach… I dried my eyes and put it back. Then I left the house to visit the site. I couldn't let it remain a hole in your history or a stain on the map.

A truck. It slams past, its sides rippling, frisky, as though pleased to leave the speed limit and run free. Never mind me, buffeted by its backdraught like the tousled nettles.

That first, bright morning, the trucks had roared behind me, stalking me like huge beasts, but I'd seen only the road like a strip of lead stretching into the liquid distance. Each stride sliced the air, snipped the tarmac. I was scratched by the hawthorn hedge, and a red streak welled up on my cheek. I crossed the lanes without looking, and didn't notice the dirty, white line.

By the time I reached the ivy-covered oak, I was hot and out of breath. I heard pounding in my chest, my head. I had pictured skid marks, spray paint, pieces of shattered windscreen, and gouged earth. But all I found were fragments of grimy, grey plastic in the grass. I stood with my back to the road, planting my grief in the ditch, my thoughts of you fractured by facts from the inquest. After a while I realised that I'd been staring at the litter. A deflated plastic bag lay in a puddle of water, surrounded by old newspaper, chocolate wrappers, and cans.

Someone saw me and told the boys. That evening Robert rang to say: 'Bloody hell, Mum. Walking along the main road? Have you got a death-wish?' Ben phoned to ask if I'd gone mad. 'Please don't do that again,' he said. But I had to do something. My chest felt like a bag of stones.

Today two pheasants are sparring in the stubble field. They have white collars and tweedy feathers and, you were right: they do look like plump farmers after a boozy lunch. You hated pheasants but you always pointed them out. Once, as we drove east to the coast, we saw one which had just been run over. Another lingered nearby, strutting back and forth as though expecting its partner to get up and continue the fight. 'Stupid bird,' you huffed. But its confusion, its strange loyalty to the dead, touched you.

Listen. My pockets are chattering as though full of marbles. The click-clack of conversation. The scrape and shuffle of company.

Oh, don't be stupid… Don't do it… You haven't time… There's something coming.

Brake! Brake! Brake!

For God's sake! So close… Could've wiped us all out... Tossers!

Keep walking, Victoria. Nearly there.

On your last day the autumn sun was low. It gleamed on the wet road as you headed home. Were you singing? I expect so, the speakers trembling as the aria saturated the space and seeped through the thin, metal shell around you. You accelerated up the rise to see… What? A car slowly overtaking a tractor? Or…was it her? Boudica? Your warrior queen charging towards you, hair blazing, weapons glinting in the low light.

I heard the sirens from our house. I expected you home with your arms full of books, balancing the stack until you reached the kitchen table where you'd let them slide and fall.

One was found on the road…

Go on biker. That's it. Carve a route through my thoughts.

The plastic bag remains, unlike my flowers. I hope the daffodils return in the spring. I like to see their yellow petals flare and fade as I drive past.

I've brought you something else this year, just in case I don't walk this way again. It is not your book. Not yet. Although Robert says it's almost finished. It hasn't been easy. Boudica has proved elusive. She's refused to yield her history or appear in his dreams…

By the way, you're welcome in mine, anytime.

Here: my offering. Treasure, which has grown warm in my pockets, my palms. It is heavy. I'll put it beside the ditch.

One… two… three hag stones from Walberswick beach. Four pebbles: orange, red, green, and grey, from Dunwich, where the storm surge breached the bank. And two bone-white, black-hearted flints from the fields.

This is your cairn, my love. A bouquet of stones.

The Game Of Love!

- Holly McDede -

Congratulations on deciding to play *the Game of Love!*

Objective: To win.

What is winning? This is a good question.

Pieces include: You, someone else, and 320 self-esteem points to be equally divided among participants.

A note on self-esteem points: Use these wisely! As each self-esteem point drops, you will become less attractive and will lose another 20 self-esteem points. If you have negative self-esteem points, you will no longer exist.

Let's begin.

Roll the dice!

You are hard at work in the newspaper office. You love the news. It makes you feel like there's life beyond *the Game of Love!*

Things that are happening: Ukraine accuses Russian troops of attacking its forces. Stephen Fry shares photos of a wedding cake. Researchers discover an environmental use for drones. And, wouldn't you know it, in Slovakia the real lottery prize goes to the tax man!

You are too engrossed in the world to notice the boy, who works in advertising, sitting next to you. Then one day, he says, 'Hello.'

You do not hear him. He says it louder, 'Hello! Hello! Hello!'

The boy notices that you do not notice him, and wants you more. You notice him noticing you not noticing him.

Move forward 20 spaces.

He moves back 30 spaces.

Do you accept your opponent?

You accept.

Continue to ignore him for the next three rounds. It'll leave him drooling. Please draw an *Advice* card.

Your *Advice* card says:

'Sitting in a room full of guys? Turn sideways in your chair, cross your legs, arch your back, and run your fingers through your hair. Pick up a pair of silk boxers on the ground and say to your opponent, 'Hey, did you leave these in the office last night?'

Your opponent looks confused.

Move back 10 spaces. Oh well, some guys just can't take the hint.

You draw a *Casual Work Place Banter* card. Please exchange Casual Banter for the next three rounds.

'Casual banter,' you say.

'Casual banter,' he says.

You discuss the news, absent-mindedly. 'Hey,' he notes. 'A child was hit by a falling loudspeaker at Bewilderwood in Hoveton.'

You offer your own contribution. You declare, 'Two stags and a herd of hinds went for a dip to cool down in the lake at Snettisham Park as temperatures soared!'

'Oh, really? So what are your hobbies?' he asks. 'What is your name?'

You inform him you cannot give him this information. He informs you that you are mysterious. You laugh. You go, 'Ha!' He goes, 'Hahahahaha!'

'Everything is so much fun,' he says, and then, 'You smell so nice.'

You proceed to discuss the news, declaring, 'Antarctica's ice losses have doubled!'

You remain on the same space for the next 43 days.

Let's get this ball rolling, please. As you've just heard, Antarctica's ice losses have doubled.

You send him an email.

Your email reads:

Local Woman Invites Local Man to Subway!

Hello, Opponent. Want to go to Subway tomorrow? It is a pun on the subway transportation system and the pathway to God. Would you like to go with me?

He walks over to your desk. 'Hey,' he says. 'Subway sounds like a lot of fun.

I didn't think you liked me all that much, so this is really awesome. Thank you!'

Is your opponent feeling okay? Why does he sound so honest, so sincere? Has he never played the *Game of Love!* before?

Numbers are exchanged. Pizza is eaten. More casual banter.

'Casual banter,' you say.

'Casual, casual banter,' he says.

'Profits fall at Marks and Spencers,' you tell him. 'UK housing prices up 8% in a year.'

'Oh really?' he asks. 'Where is your house?'

'It's right next door, actually,' you say. 'Would you like to come over?'

He comes over.

Please draw a *Sex!* card.

You have *Sex!* Congratulations.

You both must now draw your *History* cards.

History Cards

1. You majored in Journalism and it saved your life

2. Your parents have had an unhealthy marriage of silence

3. Your heart has been broken every 60 days for the past 12 years by opponents in *the Game of Love!*

4. If you are able to obtain your partner's *History* cards, you may move 350 points up

'Can I see your *History* cards?' he asks.

'Can I see yours?' you fire back.

He hands them to you. You read them to yourself. Your opponent has:

1. had a healthy, functional childhood

2. fallen in love once (with Taylor Swift when he was sixteen)

3. experienced the death of two Chihuahuas

4. experienced almost nothing at all

You ask him, 'What is your favorite food?' and then, 'What are your hobbies?' and then, 'When was the first time someone broke your heart with their bare hands?'

When he finishes writing you his autobiography, you conclude the evening by shouting, 'You're hired!'

You draw another *Sex!* card. You draw 12 sex cards.

'I really, really, really like you,' he says one evening.

You are winning by a lot. He asks for your *History* cards once more. You say you don't have any history. Who needs history? Every day is the first day of your life!

The Texting Round

You have now entered *Texting World!* It is a world inhabited only by text messages. All the food is baked in text message sauce, all the emotions are made of text messages.

Oh! You've just received a text. Please open your text.

Hi Lucy, how's your day going?

You've just gained five self-esteem points.

Please note: The amount of time you take to respond to his text message must be double the time he took to respond to yours. He takes 5 minutes. You take 10. He takes 1. You take 2. He takes 10 seconds. It's getting a little out of hand. You feel like you are drowning. Take 2 days. Move forward 200 spaces.

The Real Life Interaction Round

One day, you and your opponent are lying in bed together. Stroke his back. Tell him – 'You remind me of my cat.' There is no better way to make a guy feel like you don't take him all that seriously than to tell him you remind him of your cat, especially when you don't even have a cat. Your opponent demands your *History* cards once more. You examine them in your hands.

In Depth History Cards

1. February, 2010, 7:34pm: Your first boyfriend, Mark Zader, tells you he and his family have decided to move away to Detroit tomorrow. He does not move away to Detroit, ever. You see him at Tesco's the next day. He confesses he didn't know how to tell you that he broke up with you so he could date Mindy Chaser instead

2. That was 7 years ago

3. If Mark Zader never actually broke up with you, perhaps you are still dating. Perhaps you are cheating on Mark Zader with your opponent

'Have you ever been in love?' your opponent asks.

You laugh.

'Can I see your *History* cards?' he asks.

'What kind of music do you listen to?' he asks.

Warning, warning! Hide, hide!

'You know,' you say. '50s music.'

'Like what?' he presses. 'You mean, like Elvis?'

'No, I mean, like, Green Day,' you say. 'Anyway, do we have to talk about ourselves? Isn't that a little overrated? Let's communicate with silence.'

There is a long silence.

He drives home, listening to Taylor Swift, wondering what the room tone of your soul sounds like. He is dramatic like that. He texts you. You ignore him. He texts you. You ignore him. He says hello to you at work. You say hello back. You haven't been looking so hot at the work place lately. It's like you've forgotten all about the news. Games are more fun than the news.

Welcome to the Drunk Text Message World!

Life has turned into a drinking game. Would you like to send a drunk message? Here's some to choose from!

1. Just went to the bathroom at the [bar/party/restaurant] and took off everything, but left something special on for you

2. Oh god I am soooooo drunk!!!! Can u come in heer and help me find the door :)))

3. Using 1 handto rite this txt (sorry 4 typos!!) & press the Send button. Using the other ahnd to presh MY butt...

But instead you send him this: I am sorry. I am an idiot. He texts you back: It's okay. I understand.

You select an *Emotion Card*. Uh-oh, you are about to feel:

1. Longing

2. Regret

3. Like throwing the whole game out your window and going to his house

and apologizing

You text him: I'll be right over.

Please go back 80spaces.

He texts you back: Finally.

You sit down on his bed, and read him the news. 'Warm spring conditions should help Britain's rarest bumblebee as wildlife experts reintroduce a new batch of queens to help boost the species,' you say. 'Also, I am sorry for ignoring you. I have a problem.'

You lay down next to him.

You move back 1234 spaces.

You give your opponent a tour of your childhood by showing him your house on Google Maps. You tell him, 'I don't actually like 50s music. Actually, maybe I do. I don't know if I've ever heard 50s music.'

He asks for your *History* cards.

You give him every last one of them.

He kisses you, and holds up the *Game of Love!* by its throat.

'We should burn it,' he says.

You agree, but can't find any fire.

Soon you find yourself responding to his text messages without any hesitation, frying Pork Gammon for him on your George Foreman Grill, listening to his doubts and insecurities well into the night. You talk about the coup in Thailand, the Kidney dialysis machine for babies, and plans to cut hospital admissions. When you are finished, you tell him your name. It's a bit late for that, but better late than never, right? You tell him your fears, your hopes, your weaknesses, news of your family, news of your life. He tells you his.

One day, he tells you he is going to visit his brother in Michigan.

'Michigan?' you say.

Did he not even *read* your *History* cards? You will not fall for it again. You take the *Game of Love!* out of your closet.

You consult your weapons:

1. Self doubt

2. A lonely ex-boyfriend

3. A live streamed baseball game

4. A box of chocolates

You're going to use them all.

You walk to Mark Zader's house. Or, his parent's house, where he still lives.

'Hello,' you tell him. 'I found this box of chocolates and was wondering if it was yours.'

'Lucy?' he says. 'Wow, I haven't seen you in a while! Are you okay?'

'Yes,' you say. 'I just wanted someone to watch the baseball game with.'

He tells you to come on in. You watch the A's game.

The 7th inning arrives. The pitcher throws another baseball. The batter does not hit the baseball. The batter hits it. Someone catches it. Mark Zader puts his arm around you. The pitcher throws the ball. Mark Zader strokes your thigh. The pitcher throws the ball. The batter misses the ball. The pitcher throws the ball. Baseball is very exciting.

'I want to see how it ends,' Mark Zader says. 'There's only nine innings, right?'

'If no one scores anything by the ninth inning,' you say. 'They just keep going.'

'You're kidding!' he shouts. 'What if no one scores anything ever?'

He is so disheartened by the possibility that someone may never score that he decides to take it upon himself to get the ball rolling, so to speak. He hits a home run! Going, going, going, gone.

After the crowd applauds wildly and the game ends, he tells you to get dressed.

'I'd drive you home,' he says. 'But I'm tired, and I don't like driving when I'm tired. It gets me all confused, you know?'

You go back to your opponent's house. He smiles when he sees you. You run to the toilet, use your *Phone a Friend* card, and give Paul, a former opponent in the *Game of Love!*, a ring.

'Hey, Paul,' you say. 'It's me, Lucy.'

'Oh, good,' he says. 'What's up?'

'I'm losing,' you say. 'There's this guy. He's sweet and honest and I really like him. So I got scared and I went to Mark Zader's house.'

'Great,' he says. Sounds perfect.'

'No, it's awful! Because I only did it because I like him and I'm scared,' you say. 'But he's still 3204 spaces ahead of me and I only have 1 self-esteem point left. Do you have any advice?'

'It's not a game,' he says, uselessly.

'Don't tell me that,' you say. 'If it's not a game that means it matters.'

You hang up the phone, and walk to the boy waiting for you in the living room. You roll the dice.

Falling

- Jane Martin -

Liam was out of bed again. Sasha could hear the rumble of his toy cars on the bare boards of the kids' room. Bloody Mark and his lame promises. When Mark told Liam to go to bed he listened. None of them messed with their dad. Sasha pressed her hands over her ears, screwed her eyes tight shut. She couldn't face another battle. She just couldn't. If she went up he'd throw a tantrum and wake the others. One hand strayed unconsciously from her ear to her ribs, still bruised and tender from his flailing fists, the other reached for her glass. At least now he was calm. So what if he'd be tired in the morning. Let the school deal with that.

Sasha reached for the vodka. No lemonade left. Kaya had knocked the bottle out of her hands earlier. Nearly full too. At least it wasn't the vodka. She'd jumped up, shouting, as the bottle emptied itself into the armchair, making it reek like an old, wet dog. It wasn't her fault Kaya smacked her head on the table. Not that bloody Michelle would see it that way. To Michelle it was just another cross in another box, but for Sasha it was one step closer to losing her kids. Her precious babies, sure they drove her mad sometimes but that's what kids do. She remembered how she and her brother had made their mum crazy. Still did. But it didn't stop her loving them. And Sasha loved her kids, she loved them so much it filled an aching pit inside her. She didn't have the words to explain. She couldn't make Michelle understand that it didn't matter if she shouted at Kaya, it didn't matter if she slapped Liam's legs when the little sod kicked her, it didn't even matter if little Ryan had to wait until they could go shopping for his nappy to be changed. They were family. They loved her and she loved them and they knew it.

It was OK neat, Sasha thought. She took a long drink and waited for her thoughts to fall silent, for the world to retreat. She longed for the easy oblivion of her teenage years, when a bottle of cheap wine and a straw would get her pissed before a night out. Her and Chelsea getting dressed up, giggling, excited. Getting ready was often more fun than the club. Then she met Mark. Another swig. Why, oh why, did every thought she had bring her back to him? Her lovely Mark. That smile. It still made her insides tingle even after eight years and three kids. The tears crawled silently down her face. The time for sobbing was long gone. She had no energy for that. She poured vodka onto the livid wound of Mark's betrayal.

Liam's play was getting louder. The longer she left him, the more confident he was growing. She'd have to go up. But not yet. She'd have this drink first. Sasha sat staring at the floor, motionless, the glass with the last of the vodka clutched protectively to her chest. Her eyes no longer registered the stains, intense against the faded carpet. Her mind was quieter now, the vodka working its magic. Sometimes she thought she'd got it, the right words for the people who were shaping her life. She'd practise them over and over until she had the chance to speak. Then, as she opened her mouth, they turned to mist and she breathed them out into nothingness. The crater they left became clogged with a stir-fry of half-sentences and, as she desperately tried to unscramble them, she could hear her voice filling the silence. Fear was driving the wrong words out of her. She was like a cornered animal snapping and snarling, defensive, aggressive. Inside her head she was howling 'Nooooo' but she couldn't find a way to stop, to change direction, to explain how she really felt. All they saw was a foul-mouthed, cocky know-it all…Dr Durrant…Michelle…Liam's school…and Mark. Even her Mark. Why couldn't they see how much she needed their help? Instead they criticised and got impatient when she didn't make changes. She wasn't helping herself, they said. Did they think she liked living in a dirty, chaotic battleground? But she didn't know how to change things. She was drowning and they just tutted and walked away. They didn't even try to hide their contempt. Even her lovely Mark. Eventually.

Liam was making car noises. He knew she couldn't force him to go to bed so why should he give a shit about making a noise? They said he'd grow out of the temper tantrums. Terrible twos, they called it. Now he was six they called it ADHD. She could deal with it when he was two and he was the only one. Then Kaya came along and he got worse. Or maybe he just got bigger, stronger. Mark could handle him. He'd hold him still, whispering calmly in his ear, until the rage seeped away. The medicine helped. When she could get him to take it. She had to open the capsule and mix the powder with something he liked. Trouble was one day he liked strawberry yoghurt. Then he didn't. Sometimes he'd eat ice-cream. Sometimes he wouldn't.

Sasha drained her glass and balanced it on a pile of unopened post, letterbox-crumpled flyers and free papers. Standing – lightheaded, swaying – she reached for the wall, the chair back, the table. Progress through the minefield of plastic toys was slow, their vivid colours mocking her with promises of innocent joy.

As Sasha started up the stairs, Liam fell silent. Then a wail. Kaya. Sasha reached the bedroom. Liam was on the bottom bunk, astride his sister, driving his toy truck over her face. Thank God. Kaya wasn't hurt. Ryan, awake now too, stood up in his cot, nappy half off, lip trembling.

'LIAM, what the fuck are you doing?' Sasha leaned in and snatched the truck. Liam screamed, holding on tightly. 'LET GO, Liam. Kaya, stop it. You're not hurt.' As Sasha pulled away she whacked the back of her head on the top bunk.

'SHIT!' exploded Sasha, clutching her head and releasing the truck. As Liam catapulted backwards, his truck bashed Kaya's nose. She screamed. Liam's head hit the wall with an almighty CLONK. His yells joined with his sister's. Ryan sat and rocked, whimpering. The miasma of soiled nappy invaded the room.

And something broke.

Sasha felt it growing in her core, boiling and rising, spreading, cutting through the vodka-blur. Sasha was anger. She grabbed Liam's feet and dragged him out of Kaya's bunk. He tried to hold on but Sasha had taken him by surprise and the strength of this anger knew no limits. He fell to the floor, screaming as his head and torso thump onto the bare wood. Sasha was yelling, her throat ripping with the force of the words, her face almost purple. No-one in the room knew what she was saying. Especially not Sasha.

She dropped Liam's feet and yanked him by the arms. He was standing now, tears of terror dampening his Spiderman pyjama top, as his mum's boozy breath blasted his face. He put his arms up to fend off the rain of blows. Then she lifted him roughly and threw him up onto his bunk. The door slammed.

Sasha stumbled down the stairs, every cell in her body was shaking. Halfway down her legs gave way and she slid in to a heap by the front door. She could hear all three kids crying, but the rage had gone leaving a void where her emotions should be. Horror trickled down her spine, filling the emptiness drip by drip. She couldn't breathe. Despair hit like a tsunami. What was she going to do? Michelle would have the kids taken off her for sure now. They'd be split up. Sent miles away. She couldn't let that happen. Mark. She must speak to Mark. Now. Mobile. Where was her mobile? It didn't matter. She hadn't had credit for a week.

Sasha strayed into the night, door left gaping. Mark. He'd be with HER, Sasha's lip curled at the thought. Couldn't be helped. This was about the kids. She would make him understand. It wasn't about the two of them anymore, if he didn't want to be with her, then, OK, she'd find a way to deal with that but he needed to be there for the kids. She couldn't do it on her own. It wasn't safe.

Sasha ordered her thoughts as she walked, got the words ready, swept away the images of Mark and HER that scuttled across her mind. There it was. The house he shared with Rachel 'spread 'em' Jones. The nausea rolled around her insides like thunder. Three deep breaths and she rang the doorbell. She waited then held her finger on the button. She heard the long, insistent trill then the sound of feet on stairs. The door opened.

'Oh for God's sake!' Rachel glowered, 'What the hell do you want? It's the middle of the bloody night. Piss off.' Rachel started to close the door. Sasha pushed past her.

'What the fuck do you think you're doing? Get out!' Rachel grabbed Sasha, manhandling her towards the door. Sasha resisted, shouting,

'Mark. MARK. Get off me you bitch, I need to talk to Mark.'

'Leave her, Rach,' said Mark coming up behind Rachel. He rested his hand reassuringly on her back. Sasha saw and the wound inside her tore open again. She knew this touch. It meant, 'don't worry, I'm here. Everything will be OK.'

'What's going on, Sasha? Where are the kids? You've not left them on their own?' Mark asked, concern lying in wait beneath his irritation.

'They're…they're at home. They're fine…well…sort of…' The words robbed Sasha's mouth of moisture. She swallowed. 'Mark, I need you, I can't do this on my own. I can't cope. The kids…they're too much. You have to be there.

They need a dad. I…I…I can't…' Her carefully planned sentences broke apart, the words clambered over each other before collapsing in a heap, topped by Sasha's wracking sobs.

'We've been through this. I'm not coming back. Jesus Christ! It's the middle of the night. You've got to stop, Sash. It's not doing anyone any good.' He doesn't shout, nor does he comfort. His words are controlled, distant. He holds the door open. Sasha hesitates then leaves.

'You need help. Honest to God you do.' Mark shakes his head, bewildered by this wreck of a woman he used to love. 'I'll be round Saturday for the kids.' The door closes.

Walking head down, unseeing, all words have fled; memories slideshow through her mind: Mark. Dancing. Laughing. Mark's eyes locking onto hers as their bodies met in shared passion. Mark with the babies, new-born and fragile in his strong hands. Mark playing footie with Liam, tickling Kaya, lifting Ryan high above his head. Then Mark in bed with HER. Laughing. At Sasha. Then kissing and…Sasha forced her mind to black. She must focus on herself, on the kids. She saw her home, the untidy clutter, the chores waiting to be done, the dirt. The unopened post, full of bills she couldn't pay and threats she couldn't handle. She felt her shoulders sag with the weight of a life she wasn't strong enough to live. Finally, she saw the kids' room. Their scared, tear smudged faces, Ryan's dirty nappy. The bruises.

The enormity of it all punched Sasha in the gut. She doubled over, throat burning as she showered the road with vodka. Sasha hunched on the cold kerb, her face in her hands, rocking. She couldn't do this anymore. She couldn't watch them take her children. Without them and Mark there was no point. Better if she went. Clean. Maybe Mark would…no, not while he was with HER. She'd already had HER kid put into care.

The movie in her mind resumed.

Liam: Constantly in trouble at school and his foster home, angry, defensive, aggressive. Unloved, unlovable. Like her. She saw him shoplifting, drinking and fighting. Blood. Prison.

Kaya: Desperate for love and attention. Foster father in her bedroom. Abusive boyfriend. Pregnant. Too much, too young. Like her.

Ryan: Rows of coloured bricks. Silent. Distant eyes. Doctors. Tests. Different. Bullied. Lonely, trapped inside himself. Like her.

She couldn't leave them. No. They would go together. Somewhere better. Happy. Free.

Sasha stood. Everything was clear now.

The house. The stairs. The bedroom. Sleeping. Good. Soft kisses. Smiling. Gentle tears of love. Pillow.

Outside. Running now, anxious to join her babies. Together forever. Stairs. Up, up, up. From the car park roof, Sasha turned away from the sad, little town below her towards the sea. As the first tendrils of the new day reached over the horizon, arms wide, head back, she was flying.

Did You Eat Lunch?

- Hannah Garrard -

The man in the white apron plates mussels outside the Korean shellfish barbeque restaurant —*jogae gui*. I'd spot him most mornings, through the narrow gap between the cold noodle take-away and The Seaman's Club, or in the evenings on my way to Baskin Robbins' ice-cream parlour.

I filmed the shellfisher one afternoon, his consent given by a cursory nod, cracking and splitting shells: mussels the length of your hand, clams as wide as your palm. His deft knife-work is lascivious: twist, crack, split, twist, crack, split. We exchange smiles on most occasions, sometimes a perfunctory Korean greeting. But too many distractions might send the knife plunging deep into the flesh of his ungloved hand. So I walk quickly on.

It took me a year to go into his restaurant and eat; I needed a dinner date who'd know what to do. Korean barbeque rituals are learned as you grow up. You listen to your parents judging the heat by the colour of the embers; they tell you the grill is not hot enough because the air above it does not wobble. They snatch your hand away if you lean in too close and scold you so you'll learn. At twenty-nine, I was a *jogae gui* virgin.

When mussels and other molluscs are condemned to the grill, they reveal their secret weapon, their one and only act of insubordination: self-annihilation. 'Quick! Take it off before the clam explodes!' my dining companion commands. I lift the mollusc with the tongs, but am too late and shards of shell shrapnel discharge themselves, narrowly missing my face.

I have burnt the largest mussel on the grill—The Daddy—that the shellfisher had ceremoniously presented at our table. A white plastic bucket sits beneath each round, galvanized barbeque station—a graveyard for the spoiled—into which the blackened shell and its curled, dead remains are thrown. A group of middle-aged men talk loudly and jovially over one another through mouthfuls of shellfish as the air greys with their cigarette smoke. Steadily emptying green bottles of *soju*—rice wine—clutter their table.

I am still hungry.

At the barbeque station next to us is a well-dressed couple; the red in his check shirt is striking against her livid-green blouse. She is in charge of the grilling and the monitoring. He leans his upper body to the left—still talking—in anticipation of a shellfish-seizure. She whips a clam off the grill with tongs, scoops the torpid contents out with a pair of silver chopsticks, delivers a smudge of red *gochujang* (hot pepper sauce) and places it, delicately, into her boyfriend's mouth.

I wore a hairy jumper to dinner and stray fibres keep catching in the heat as I reach across the grill with my tongs. Small, transitory fires on my clothes add to the anxiety of eating *jogae gui*.

Across the road from the *jogae gui* restaurant, where an evangelical church with shepherds and cartoon lambs on its double-doors faces the street, is the Bonjuk restaurant—a franchise selling healthy Korean cuisine.

I don't have to prepare my seafood here.

The day after a shard of shark fin-shaped glass went into my hand and I needed twelve stitches, I went into Bonjuk alone for the first time. I was so grateful for good food you could eat one-handed with a spoon. All the dishes came in large, stone bowls: soups, porridge, *bibimbap*, and *gul juk gui*—spicy oyster soup with glass noodles.

Bonjuk saw me through those one-handed weeks.

Sinpo was my neighbourhood in Incheon—my city by the sea for two years. And you could eat fresh oysters anywhere. Bonjuk restaurants only sell the *gul juk gui* where oysters are in abundance; the empty shells sound like castanets as they are scraped from the bowl and tumble into the bin.

The first time I ate at Bonjuk the waitress, a woman in her middle years with admirable posture, looked warily at my bandaged hand and asked me if I was meeting someone. 'I'm on my own,' I told her. One other lone diner was sat in the middle of the restaurant at a beige Formica table. The waitress laid a place in front of him, took my elbow and guided me into the seat opposite. He looked up, startled by the bandaged foreign woman (Russian? Strips at The Seaman's Club?). Embarrassed, I insisted I was content to eat alone.

Gul juk gui was a lucky guess; I could read Korean well enough but the nuances of heat, the type of dish it's served in, and many vegetables were still a mystery. Oyster soup could be anything. A portion could feed two, but I always emptied the bowl. Most of it could be eaten one-handed with a spoon; the noodles with flat chopsticks, *ideally* with two hands, coiling the noodles into the spoon. Bite down hard on the oysters—they're more resistant than you think— and their rubbery skins give, releasing a briny piquancy that mingles with the fieriness of the soup and conjures the sea.

The side dishes that come with each Korean meal are little bowls of colourful promise: pickled ribbons of deep green seaweed and hot-pink slices of radish. Along with the oysters, *gul juk gui* gave me all my iron and zinc. I needed to heal; I'd lost a lot of blood when I cut my hand.

But it would have been nice to share *gul juk gui* with someone.

Jae-ik and I met at Culture Complex—the language exchange centre where he was the manager. I liked his thick glasses and sticky-out hair. When I explained the unfortunate name for his language programme, he laughed, and wrote it down in his pocket-notebook under 'homonyms'.

Our first date was a traditional Korean meal with all the side dishes carefully displayed in jade ceramics—*banchan*. I asked him lots of questions about the technique, the history and the legends behind everything we were eating: Korean kingdoms adopted Buddhism as its state religion, and court kitchens cultivated elaborate ways to prepare simple, Buddhist dishes. My favourite was the miniature *kimchi* pancakes.

Jae-ik said that he found my appetite charming.

The bus on the way home was crammed with commuters so we had to stand, swaying unsteadily into one another as it charged around corners. He ran an index finger along the inside of my wrist, and whispered something in my ear.

Jae-ik's first gift to me was a can of pomegranate juice from the 7/11. 'It's good for women—for *down there*,' he said, offering it to me with both hands like it was an injured bird.

Jae-ik liked to eat Korean beef barbeque—*bulgogi*. One evening he sprung it on me that I was to meet his *hyun*, a respected older male friend, and that we'd all eat *bulgogi* together. Jae-ik was his *dong-saeng*, and therefore required approval from his mentor over his choice of girlfriend. His *hyun* spoke elegant English, better than Jae-ik, but as the *soju* flowed, the *hyun* got impatient and before too long both he and Jae- ik were talking in slurred Korean and I couldn't follow. Not trusted with the barbeque, I sat bored and mute watching the *kimchi* frying on the hotplate, the edges of each cabbage leaf blackening and spoiling, the *hyun's* cigarette ash showering the meat. The men shovelled over-done beef cuts into their mouths and then ordered *yook hwe*, a raw beef salad mixed with raw egg, and laughed when I made a face.

Jae-ik had red *gochujang* all over his chin.

On the train back to my flat, after dinner was finally over, I made Jae-ik sit with his head between his knees so he didn't puke *yook-hwe* all over the carriage. He looked up through pink eyes, and told me that he was under a lot of pressure at home to get married. 'I'm the oldest son,' he told me mournfully, 'I have to find someone soon. It might as well be you.' We argued, and then he puked in my bathroom. His final gift to me was an ugly pair of sparkly earrings, an apology that confirmed we didn't know anything about each other at all.

My apartment block straddled Sinpo and China Town, and my bedroom looked out onto the Incheon port in the East China Sea. I found it satisfying watching the sun sink at different points behind the mountains as the seasons changed. December promised the best sunset. A flash of pink and auburn on the surface of the ocean before the sun dips finally, making room for dusk to move in. Neon Hangeul signs blink to life and take over the skyline.

It was Chinese settlers who brought *Jjajangmyeon* to Korea. They landed at Incheon and set up their shops on a tiny sliver of the city about a kilometre wide. *Jjajangmyeon*—chewy noodles topped with a glutinous black soybean sauce—even has its own song. Korean kids learn it in kindergarten and needle their parents for the noodles on the weekend.

In China Town, not far from a weary-looking stone Confucius, an enormous fiberglass effigy of a bowl of *jjajangmyeon* is on display. Visitors make their pilgrimage to China Town for the day, have their picture taken with the noodles, and then eat a bowl of it in one of the ubiquitous Chinese restaurants. Outside the *Jjajangmyeon* museum, a colossal statue of a chef in whites is frozen in mid-run, clutching a take-away box of *jjajangmyeon*.

It is possible to map the evolution of Korea's cuisine against the country's own extraordinary evolution from feudal state, to military dictatorship, to capitalist democracy. Contrary to the stereotypes of an inflexible and rigid culture—it was once referred to as 'The Hermit Kingdom'—Korea has moved with the times. *Jjajangmyeon* is a perfect example of this: Koreans have selected the appetizing parts of Chinese influence and turned them into a national dish, complete with its own festival.

American influence has also had its way with Korean cuisine, and this came as a shock—when I found pieces of deep-fried Spam on my tray in the school canteen. Rows of Spam in blue and yellow tins line supermarket shelves, and are a popular gift to take home during the *Chuseok* holiday. Army Stew—a spicy (and revolting) Spam based noodle soup is sometimes called Johnson's Stew in honour of President Lyndon B. Johnson, who visited Korea in 1966 and promised economic aid. Spam, an uninviting flabby by-product of a free-market economy, has attained mythical status.

Where British custom discusses the weather in meaningless detail before easing into lucid conversation, Koreans ask about your last meal: 'Did you eat something?' is the opener for most greetings. If I said 'no,' I would be handed a snack dug out of a handbag—usually a rice cake, *tteok*. And on one occasion, when I said I had not eaten breakfast, I was marched to a nearby restaurant and forced to eat a bowl of *bibimbap*—rice and bean sprouts—until I was full, *pae-bol-oy-yo*. I soon learned that the stock answer was always 'yes,' in the same way that the British don't expect anyone to not be 'fine'.

But I never really got used to this overly personal greeting in the two years I lived in Korea. You could be hurrying past a colleague in a busy corridor, who'd meet your eye and shout, 'Did you eat lunch?' and frantically mime spooning food into their mouth, in place of a wave. There'd be no time to stop and answer, so the question was always left hanging, like an awkward expression of unrequited love. I made it my business to email the colleague who'd enquired and finish the exchange: 'Yes, I ate lunch. Thank you for asking.'

Reporter

– Radhika Oberoi –

'Don't worry, Madam; it is just a house mouse. It only stares and doesn't bite.' Nirmal Kaur spoke with the reassurance of one who had lived in fond familiarity with sewage rats. The front door of her flat was open – it stood unhinged and at a slant, as though obliged to perform the duty of a front door, despite its obvious deformity of rusty hinges.

Aradhana tried not to look at the rat. She stared, instead, at the right-angled triangle of sunlight formed by the door that leaned against a dirty-orange wall. Her notebook lay open on her lap. A cup of tea lay on the uneven floor she squatted on.

The cup was chipped in several places, and Aradhana, nervous about sipping from the jagged rim, had left the tea untouched. The rat contemplated it now, with sharp, unblinking eyes, before it scurried out of the room and into a maze of open drains, overflowing with the collective effluence of the Widows' Colony.

Aradhana composed herself for this assignment. Not that anyone at the office cared about the piece she wanted to write – the story had been reported and analysed a million times before, by seasoned journalists who had managed to give it a new angle each time. They had filed the details of a compliant history under *Special Report, Deep Focus, Wide Angle, Editorial, Opinion* and *Perspective*. What had happened here, over thirty years ago, was a meticulous butchery. But it had been presented to the world in neatly labelled packages of copy that were not too unpleasant to read on a Sunday afternoon.

She would write it differently. She would scurry through this hotchpotch of matchbox-sized flats and naked sewers, like the rat. She would talk to everyone, all three generations of traumatised victims, the ones who had witnessed it, the ones who had fled from its kerosene-soaked grip, and the ones who were born into families truncated by an inconceivable violence.

She would record every word they spoke, and make diligent notes. She would file an honest, unpretentious piece, and pay her dues to a kinder fate, that had, a long time ago, diverted the violence away from the gates of her own home.

Aradhana told herself she wouldn't care if the piece never got published, because it was a mere regurgitation of the events of one wintry season. This assignment was for her to understand. It was a shard of the past she had escaped. Back then, she had only been eight-and-a-half. A giddy witness to grown-ups talking in whispers about 'a riot somewhere'.

It was only now that she understood why her ninth birthday party had been cancelled. It had been the bloodiest day of the riot. Trilokpuri had gone up in flames. Sultanpuri had howled itself silent. Shops had been ransacked. Hair – long, dark and curly – had been set free from the turbans that marked men for slaughter, and doused in petrol.

Nirmal Kaur and the other residents of the Widow's Colony had managed to run for their lives, even as husbands and fathers and brothers were set on fire.

She had lived to retell the horrors of that winter in 1984. And now, she waited, somewhat impatient, her slim gold bangles catching the light of the afternoon sun, tinkling every time she adjusted the white chiffon dupatta that covered her head. She had spoken to journalists before, and had even appeared on national TV once. She could recount the massacre with textbook precision, without the slightest tremor in her voice. It had lost its grip on her, the horror of running through a street strewn with bodies, her feet squelching on fresh blood. She had held her son in her arms as she ran. He had been forced into a frock, and his long hair, usually knotted up over his head in a tight bun, had been uncoiled and plaited like a school girl's braids. The mob had been on a killing spree, lynching the menfolk or burning them alive, screaming, 'Not a single son of a Sikh will be spared.' And the only way to save the boys was to dress them up like girls and escape through dark alleys to safer parts of the city.

But that was a long time ago. She had managed to build a life for herself, in the jostling intimacy of this resettlement colony. A community of widows and orphans, recovering from collective grief. A kinship grew of a necessity to fill the cavernous emptiness. Childhoods were peopled with uncles and aunts borrowed from fuller families in the neighbourhood. Birthdays and festivals were celebrated with a firm togetherness, to populate the parties and make up for the absent.

Nirmal Kaur wondered how long the interview would take. This journalist (was she a trainee?) looked hopelessly unprepared. She had looked suspiciously into her teacup once or twice, and put it down without sipping the tea that Nirmal Kaur's daughter-in-law had prepared with cardamoms and a little extra milk. She had stared at the cracks in the wall, the stains on the divan – the only bit of furniture in the living room – and had almost fainted at the sight of a tiny rat.

Nirmal Kaur was offended. There was work to be done – peas to be shelled for the afternoon meal and lice to be removed from her grandson's tangled mass of hair. And she wasn't convinced that this journalist (what was her name again?) with her dangly silver earrings and fancy notebook could ever know what it was like to witness a husband being doused with oil and burnt alive. To witness bodies being loaded in trucks – chachas and maamas and kakas stashed upon one another like sacks of rotting grain – and driven into an oblivion.

'Hurry up madam,' said Nirmal Kaur with as much politeness as she could muster, 'Please ask me your questions. But first tell me – did you Google *1984 Sikh riots* before coming here, or no?'

The newsroom was a bustling hive of reporters and editors. And the Chief-of-City-Pages was about to self-combust. An important story had broken its shell and spilled the fresh yolk of a scoop on the dreary face of this city, and he needed a reporter to cover it. Where was that new recruit, that Special Correspondent with no regular beat or imminent deadline on her horizon?

'Aradhana!' he hollered, to her empty swivel chair. Where was she, when he finally needed her to write something of import? Probably out on some silly, self-assigned story with zero newsworthiness. He would shelve it, he thought, as anger coursed through his veins and choked a pivotal artery; he would shelve her story without reading it. How dare she disappear without a word, in the middle of a working day, when there were stories erupting on every street corner?

There were other reporters he could send, to cover this vital piece of news.

The crime reporter, for instance, that quiet, meticulous guy who could burrow deep into the recesses of a story, to cull the facts from the muck of rumour and conjecture. But this wasn't a crime piece, and the reporter wasn't much of a writer; he was too matter-of-fact, and the story that needed to be covered had to be written with depth and feeling. Not *too much* depth and feeling – Aradhana had to be ticked off constantly, to curtail her unnecessary flow of words that *felt too much, told too little* – but a small quantity of 'decent writing, Convent-style' would do for this piece.

The Chief-of-City-Pages contemplated his meagre staff. He could send someone from the environment beat. After all, this story could be written with an environmental peg. A local politician had erected a statue of herself in a public park – she was notorious for getting plump bronze lookalikes of herself built in places of beauty and relaxation. This particular statue – sixteen-feet in height, and a careful replica of her abdominal flab and double chin – had, by some miscalculation, been erected right in the middle of a joggers' lane. The joggers had formed a union and staged a protest outside the politician's home in Lutyens' Delhi.

Other newspapers had already sent reporters to talk to the joggers, the local authorities that had allowed the construction of the statue in its current awkward location, and even the politician. The Chief-of-City-Pages was on the verge of a fresh bout of rage, when Aradhana appeared at her desk, her digital camera slung across her shoulders, her notebook choking with a story that needed immediate telling.

'Where have you been,' growled the Chief-of-City-Pages.

'I've just met Nirmal Kaur, survivor of the '84 riots. Met her neighbours too, at the Widows' Colony. Need to do this story…' she mumbled.

Her editor interrupted her with his usual dose of bile. 'Need to? You *need to* do a story that has been done a million times before? The city is on the verge of collapse, we're dealing with irritated joggers and megalomaniac politicians here, we're looking at a new story that makes for good copy – if you write it decently – and it gives you a credible byline, and all you do is dig into the filth of the past, like a ratty brat? '84 is dead girl, it isn't news that sells, look around you; we are in 2014. Get a grip, girl, and grab a pen. Need to brief you on your new assignment, now.'

The black-and-white TV set had arrived in Nirmal Kaur's home with much fanfare. The first of its kind in Sector 32, Trilokpuri, it had caused an out-of-season Diwali in the neighbourhood. Crackers were burst upon its arrival and sweets were distributed in the neighbourhood.

Nirmal Kaur, a lissom nineteen year old, was fascinated by the grainy images of men and women who seemed to live their lives inside the box. They sang and danced around rose bushes, spoke animatedly about the merits of Nirma Washing Powder, Prestige Pressure Cooker and Lux Soap. Sometimes, they read the news. Nirmal Kaur was riveted by the female newsreaders, who wore a different sari every day. She wondered about the colours of the saris and assigned them one from her own palette – Turmeric Yellow, Gulmohar Orange-Red, Eucalyptus Green, Sparrow Grey, and Pigeon Blue.

On the first of November, the mob entered Sector 32, baying for the blood of Sikh men. Nirmal Kaur's sixteen-year-old brother-in-law was the only one in the family who wasn't six feet tall, as yet. He was bundled into the wooden cabinet that housed the new TV set. Its sliding doors were shut and the family prayed to their beloved Guru – the silent one who watched from afar as his sons were murdered – that it would prove to be a safe hiding place.

That was where they looked first. The memory hit Nirmal Kaur like the sword they had used to slash the cabinet, till blood had oozed out of it, and the muffled wailing inside it had been stilled.

She chose not to describe the TV cabinet massacre to Aradhana. It would be too much gore for a girl who couldn't sip tea from the jagged edges of a teacup. Besides, the day was slipping away rapidly. Her son, who, like her, had survived, would be home soon, demanding lunch.

Now You See Me

– Marise Mitchell –

Now you see me - now you don't.

I am adrift on this new stomach made of blancmange and my hair is thin at the front and thick at the back. When did that happen? I get down on the Pilates mat and wonder: will I get up again? I feel foxy fading away and it panics me. I see the young girls walking with their long limbs and straightened hair but they do not see me. A friend takes me in hand and soon I have a wildly expensive magenta colour, a push-up bra and black kinky boots. I squeak around the house but the bra is cutting in, leaving red crescents underneath my breasts, and my heels are hurting big time. I do not recognise myself in the mirror until I'm back in soft pyjamas and my wolf slippers and my hair is hurriedly coloured dark again from a Superdrug box. 'It is not over yet,' my cross friend says, swaying on her heels, rubbing Savlon on my red raw skin.

Because *it* is not over yet I sit in front of my GP while he coughs and slides me a leaflet on vaginal atrophy or dry pussy syndrome and a prescription for a bottle of goo. Because *it* is not over yet I carefully cut round a picture of Ryan Gosling and put him on the corkboard above my bed. I have to count calories now and weigh things for fear I will swell to enormous proportions and have to wear really big trousers that I can only order online from Jacamo. I walk past Zara and H&M and watch them all shopping, laughing, totally carefree, swinging their hair back over their shoulders with their teeny tiny bags on chains. Luckily they do not see me.

I fling myself around in bed. The man is impressed though a little off his stroke with Ryan Gosling looking down on us. But it helps me as does the lube. I might not be able to walk tomorrow but for now I feel a bit sexy again. I am desired and I know I am desired and that is everything. Walking around the city centre, hand in hand, my confidence is up and the world seems less slanted, somehow, less populated with people pushing past me, seeing right through me.

But when I am alone again, *when I am alone*, however much I load up my iPod with Sia and Ed and Pharrell and Paloma & co, however much I dance in my head or around the dining room table, the doubts and the fears creep back in. I feel that I have temporarily lost my place in the world and I may need to find a new one. Is this the call of the childless and the single woman echoing down through the years even when childlessness has been her choice?

I read Melanie Reid in the Saturday Times magazine and I am fired up. She would slap me and I would welcome the slap. She would challenge my introspective wallowing over *nothing*. She tells us all to be freer and be braver, not to give a damn, and I carefully snip around her words and go upstairs and add them to the corkboard above my bed. I *love* Melanie Reid.

I find biscuits really help. Ginger nuts really take the edge off and at only 45 calories each you can have quite a few. If you take the top off a custard cream it becomes two biscuits: one sweet but plain, the other with the iced cream on. 80 calories so if you snuffle down ten in one go that's it for the day and you only have enough for a very small meal. Keep away from chocolate. You don't want to go down that path; people don't come back from there. Trust me.

Because *it* not over yet and I am feeling brave I have coffee with a male student who has been giving me Mrs Robinson from The Graduate eyes and trying to impress me for weeks. He pictures me with a whip and vicious heels and Sisters of Mercy playing in the background. I know he does. I get out of breath lying to him. Yes I did live in Barcelona on my own but that was twenty years ago. I tell him five. I get twitchy because there are young girls in the corner looking over at us. I don't like cappuccino. He tries to kiss me outside, pushing me up against the dirty graffiti'd wall. I don't want *him*, I just want those years back.

He walks off and I hope to God he won't become a nuisance. Go on, I tell him, hook up with someone else. I know I can't be what he wants because it would simply be too tiring and I can't charge him, can I? When he hits 39 I will be 70 and we will be on one of those Channel 4 documentaries, me with black hair and fishnets grinning inanely at the camera with him beside me. Oh no. Better to run away now and leave him walking the long way home in his new jacket, bewildered and feeling that he has failed in spite of all his funny stories. *Sorry.*

Can someone please slap me and tell me how to negotiate this strange time ahead? I am so scared of crossing the Rubicon into the menopause. There, I've said it. So where is my guide when I need her? I see some beautiful Navajo woman clanking with beads and a heavy plait walking up to cross with me. *I can't do this on my own* I will tell her. She will nod wisely, then take me to the top of the mountain and leave me up there, cold and alone, shivering until the Emergency Services come to get me.

Counting The Pennies

– Tess Little –

NIGHT

(thck)

(thck)

(thck)

Count the pennies in my head and she'll come – thck the wall – count the pennies. Farthing, farthing, ha'penny, two. One pence, tuppence, thrup'ny bit, groat. Farthing, farthing, ha'penny –

Two. Dunt have to be a lonely soul. Stay up a while now and Anguish'll take good care of you. Lean back your head, let the walls cradle.

Like cool hands.

And dunt it thck nicely, Eliza, like patting a big, fat belly or something?

Reach out, stroking it so – up and down and thck the palm of my hand. Walk walk my fingers like little legs cross the wall-cracks, to the floor, and my feet, up my shin, top the thigh. Can see it all, even in this coal black –

You know every inch of it.

– feeling nibs with my knuckles and ridges bump my thumb. Dark all 'round me but not as a blanket. This is suffocating dark, like tumbling down deep, deep water – night dark. Seeps into clothes and clogs up my throat and slides through

166

holes of my body. Choking from inside out.

But wunt drag you down yet – these two walls, your corner, anchoring steady. Grip with your fingers… That's right. Now close your eyes – no harm when you can't see a thing – and dunt it feel safe?

What was that?

Only Sally shifting.

Not Matron?

Not Matron.

(thck)

One hand on wall, picking at the paint.

'Member you got me, Liza, keeping you safe. Keeping company. 'Member your first night? Guard dozed off. Dreamt you were drowning, woke with a heavy chest and there was Louise – crouched on top of you. Next day, what happens? Emma tries to scratch your eyeballs out and Sally in the bed along just wunt shut up talking. Asking what's your name, what you done, why you're here, and every time you dunt answer she gets closer, closer, excited, till she's whisprin in your ear *whoareyouwhoareyouwhoareyou*. And if that dint drive you mad, then it'd be Bess right opposite, humming and singing the back end off a donkey.

Can't complain, can't complain. Most of them dunt mean it. That did scare me when I arrived but used to noises now, know who to avoid –

'Cept in the nights, when the slightest thud makes you jump, crawl to your corner, and quietly thck thck thck through dark. But you've got me for company, and I'm all you need. Anguish'll take good care of you.

Clacking – is she coming for me?

Stay in your corner, Liza. I'm here and Matron wunt hurt you.

THE FOLLOWING NIGHT

(thck)

Who am I? Why here? What have I done? Pickin at the paint.

(thck)

Lodge my nail under and peel it back. This one'll be a fat flake with little chips pattering down. Dig dust from my nails. Sometimes bleeds – splinters jabbing – but no matter. Better I'm picking paint, 'stead of when I first came here, plucking eyelashes and scalp scabs. Int much else for it when you can't talk to a soul. Times like now my fingers itch to crawl under the hair… Or stroke my neck – the soft stretched… where…

(thck)

Bessie humming. Even in her sleep and always the same rhyme. *May I go with you, my pretty maid? You're kindly welcome, sir, she said. What is your fortune, my pretty maid? My face is my fortune, sir, she said.* But what's that – tapping to the beat? Clack-clack, clack-clack. Farthing, farthing, ha'penny, two. One pence –

Matron int coming in, Liza – listen to the steps fade.

But she'll be back soon.

(thck)

My poor Eliza…

Not the poorest, Anguish.

No?

No. Not by far. Know where I am, where I came from. These girls wunt know a mirror if they smacked into one. Most sit weeping, 'cept Lucy who screams and flails her arms every time Matron wakes her. You can pass round these wretches in this chicken coop and not collect a shilling between them.

Servant, servant, couple of dollymops, jemmies and a governess thrown in for good measure – but you are a poor creature too, aintcha, Eliza?

That's what they loved, those gentlemen. That's what they loved about us. Barely-five-foot waif with ragamuffin-brown hair. *My delicate little pauper. Woeful, lost soul.* Gave it all you got, dint you, Anguish?

Cough a bit, sniff a bit, cry a bit. Count the pennies. Let 'em stroke your hair for a few bob and they loved that – looking after you.

You looked after me.

Eliza, tell me the story? Tell me again.

How I found Anguish?

Go on. Tell it.

Must've been not sixteen at the time. Living in Ma's down Providence Place. One grotty room for six of us and a family next door what used to keep a pig. Disgusting. Stank through the walls, I swear, and *squealsquealsqueal.* Couldn't tell what was their babe screaming and what was that wretched animal. But weren't the only noise, course there was the family above and –

'Member the back alley? How brawls from the Pleasant Cock used to spill over?

You'd hear shoutin and cursin echo cross the cobbles. Smashing glass. Sometimes in the house too. When Ma'd bin at the bottle it was all *Jesus-Mary-and-FUCKING-Joseph, Eliza, you shitweasel, you cunt, you fucking lazy…*

And that was why you needed me.

Because it was her what pushed me into the business.

And the business pushed you to me. Go on, Eliza, tell it.

Not sixteen at the time, and working on Uncle's fish stall. Hated it. Only allowed to keep a penny off each I sold but that summer nobody fancied them half-baked, rotting-in-the-sun stinkers. Came home Saturday with not-a-penny and Ma'd drank every last farthing we had. Problem was rent were due Tuesday and landlady wunt too favourable – already owed last month's. Not that Ma took charge –

That bitch.

– thought it were straight up my fault. *Lazy Eliza,* she called me, *you ungrateful sod, where's my money?* Course she wunt having any of it when I showed an empty palm. Afore I took off my boots she was squawking, *Who do you bloody well think you are, you shitweasel, coming home with not-a-penny?* Propped up 'gainst the wall as she hobbled over, burped all the while: *Your sister works knuckle-to-the-bone sending me wages, boys doing what they can, but I'm still feedin all these mouths, still feeding lil' un and what's going to happen when we're thrown on the street? What'll happen then? What'll happen then?* Smacked the back of my head every *then.*

And she told you –

I was to get the rent money by Tuesday else that'd be the end of it. End of what? Living under her roof that's what. Course fish never could pay that kind of money, and I told her so. She said, *Well then, little missy, int it 'bout time you learnt the real world? Reckon a young thing like you can earn a few bob working the corner.*

So off you went.

Dint have one clue. I'd sin dollymops on the corner, lifting frilly skirts and leering. *Sin ya lookin sir, wunt ya like to taste a little, sir? Just a nibble, sir. Penny a nibble, sir.*

But you never were one of them ladybirds.

Couldn't do it. Realised that night – need to be loud and harsh, and little bit of Dutch courage dunt hurt. Spent few hours peering cross the road till the girls spotted and were screeching all, *What you lookin at, sunshine?*

You scarpered off.

Dint want a fight, is all. Wandered round streets watching crowds huddle card games. Bloody noses and a fair few bodies strewn 'bout the place. Dead or drunk, who knew. And for a while there I thought maybe I'd head off elsewhere, find some other job. But a waif like me couldn't last a month in the spike, doubtless where I'd end. That night I went on watching.

'Member Lady Adams?

First dollymop I saw putting a brain to use. Couldn't miss her wild ways from a mile off. Dressed in bright yellow with a doily parasol. Held it in gloved hands. Smears of dirt cross the garments but then you wunt notice for the world with her airs and graces. Attracted quite a crowd by prancing the pavement and putting on the how'd-you-do-well-to-do. Like a juggler, clown. Weren't till haggling began I even knew she were a ladybird.

And you realised there was a way to it all.

Saw how the best made their money. Hatty Wilson who treated Johns like a mother would, cuddling them up to her big, fat bosom. They called her Aunty on the streets. Hannah Pye, pretty as pansy, sat on a bench fluttering those lashes – toffs lapped it up like honey, bartering off who could take her down Gropecunt Alley for an hour. Bought her ribbons and bonnets and lollypops. And Maria, Queen of Ber Street. Rouged up her cheeks and slunk over cobbles like an eel. They say she knew all the tricks. Would have them crying out Our Lord in Heaven by the end of the night.

Then there was me – Anguish.

Course I'd heard that word often enough, Charlotte working at the Anguish Hospital. When we saw her Boxing Day she'd giggle 'bout jokes the nurses told – Anguish meaning sad and pain, they'd play suffering when Warden scolded. I thought what those good dollymops had done is use wildness what only they had. Made them something special. And what was my something special? Not a face to look at, no charm or grace. Barely-five-foot with ragamuffin-brown hair. But

Anguish –

Now that was something special.

At night, down the alley, they'd find me shivering in the corner. Gentlemen, crouching down, talking gentle. Just a waif, I was. And they'd ask my name. *Anguish*, I would whisper. Let my voice tremble oh so slight. Every time I did there'd be more to add and you – growing to a person every word I gave, every move. If I wept –

– if I held my elbows out to angle my ribcage, if I talked about the baby Jesus. *Anguish, Anguish. Anguish!* They would draw their fingers cross my cheek, tilt my chin so tears tumbled under yellow lamp-light. Best of all I did nothing. Limp, and that's how they liked me. *My delicate little pauper. Woeful, lost soul.* Cough a bit, sniff a bit, cry a bit. Count the pennies. By Tuesday I was bringing home the rent.

And Ma was chuckling as she tottered out to get her gin. *Eliza you done it, and dint I say you would? 'Bout time you learnt the real world.*

But she dint see you in the corner. Holding your legs tight as the sun rose. Crying truthful this time. Slappin that wall with the palm of your hand to make a gentle thck thck thck –

Couldn't get the shiver out my bones.

And she couldn't see me there either. Stroking you to sleep. Hushing you. *Hush Eliza*, dint I coo, *hush baby. Anguish'll take good care of you…*

(thck)

Can't get the shiver out my bones.

(thck)

(thck)

The door, Liza –

But I dint hear clacking? Can't be her.

Is her.

Matron.

"I can see you sitting awake, Eliza Bailey – your wicked eyes glint in the dark."

Sit tight, Liza. Statue, 'member? Sit tight, pull up the blanket.

"But then I suppose you like the filth, don't you?"

ANOTHER NIGHT

"Why dunt you talk, Eliza?"

Cold makes my hollow body ache. Cross hands on my chest to keep warm. Fingers on my collarbone, stroking up my neck. Skin so smooth and delicate. Not painful any more, but can feel the criss-crossing...

(thck)

"Why dunt you talk, Eliza?"

Farthing, farthing, ha'penny, two –

Sit tight, pull up the blanket. Sally will tire soon.

"Why dunt you talk?"

Her screeching, Anguish – it drives right through my skull.

'Why dunt you talk? And why you pick the walls, Eliza? Matron says picking walls is bad.'

Sit tight.

"Why do you picks walls? Eliza? Eliza? Eliza, why do you pick walls? Walls are bad, Eliza, bad picking walls, bad, wicked girl, bad, bad, badbadbadbad —"

Make it stop, Anguish —

It's stopped, you can take your hands off your ears.

Bad — am I bad? If I'm not bad, Anguish, why am I here?

(thck)

(thck)

'Member the first time you met Crow, Liza? Shook his head as he lifted your skirts, shook his head as he parted your legs. You thought he oughta pay good and proper like the rest of the Johns, and you shut your pins. Scowled. Crow laughed and said: *Consider it payment for your stay at Her Majesty's Pleasure.* You thought how it int the first time you bin told that and wunt be the last. Then he picked up his metal prod and went: *But we'll put an end all that.*

End to all what? End to the men, to life in the drum, life on the streets. Couldn't even kiss goodbye to the cobbles of Providence Place afore they whisked me to the bin. Now here I am, stuck growing old. Nothing to do with myself in here, not at all. Grey beds, sheets, walls, floor, grey faces and my grey corner. Pickin at paint.

And when you dint know what to think, he went: *But it might not be a bad prospect — three hearty meals, medical care and a roof over your head. And they say conditions have rather improved at the County Asylum.*

Then he shoved that metal bit right up there.

Got you all sudden and you shook, dint you?

Ah but weren't first time I felt it. Dint hurt. Just cold. Only shook for the cold. Lay there on the table, shivering. I dint, I dint know what to think.

So he took his metal poker out your parts — dragged right out, you could still feel the cold after — writ something down and added: *But that's for the Assize to decide.*

174

You heard the name well enough times to know it int welcome. *Assize*, Nubbiken. Remember the Nub?

Thought metal were the worst of it. Tried to sit up but Crow dint let me. That's normly the end– they've took out the prod and they've writ down then I'm back on the street. Prison, court, docs, street. Done, done, done, home.

Not this time. Put his hand on your chest to push you back down and you dint like that, did you? *Eliza*, he said. *Or Anguish, which do you prefer?*

He was laughing at us. Bastard. I shoved his hand right off me.

He sat down, sighed: *There are nevertheless some questions I must ask.* Crossed your arms, dint you Liza?

He was lookin at my neck –

He was lookin at our neck.

– and I looked him right back.

You looked him right back, you hant said a word. But Crow dint care, did he? Carried straight on.

Tapping his pen on his knee.

Stood up, lifted it to our neck –

My neck.

– and we felt the cold. *Let us begin with the ending. Why did you decide upon the rope?* Eliza, why did you decide?

Farthing, farthing, ha'penny…

Eliza, why did you…?

One pence, tuppence, thrup'ny bit…

ONE MORE NIGHT

(thck)

That time already. She's clacking, coming and jangle of keys as she – wedge of light falling on the other beds. Bodies 'neath blankets. Her shadow huffing and muttering – sin paint flakes at my toes – can't do it – Farthing, farthing, ha'penny…

Sit steady, Liza. Hands on wall.

"Eliza Bailey –"

Lantern's too bright, Anguish –

Dunt look Matron in the eye. Even now she's pinching your cheek. Keep blank.

A statue –

That's it, Liza. Play with her.

"Eliza Bailey, I don't know why it's humorous not to answer but you've been here several months and it's rude as the devil, it's quite wicked."

No, what's wicked is her foul breath – int it, Liza?

Anguish, I –

Statue, 'member? Sit tight and I'll get you through. Let's play a game.

"I can see you there – laughing behind your stony face. If you believe I can't guess what's going through your nasty, little head –"

Shilling says she never could. Because what I'm wondring is: how many seconds till she mentions Our Dear Old Lord? Go on, see if she can beat the record. One…

"– you've another thing coming, missy."

Two…

"Not spoken a word since you stepped through my doors and think you're so clever, don't you? I'll place my bets you're not missing one ounce of sanity. Might have Doctor Crawford fooled, but you can't pull the wool over my eyes –"

…Five, six…

"– so carry on being silent. Don't bother me –"

Oh she's shaking, Liza, she's shaking…

"– but the Lord knows, the Lord knows. You step one toe out of line and I shall have you in the pad, I swear, with God as my witness."

Ten seconds, ladies and gentlemen! Gets her every time. *The Lord knows, Eliza Bailey.* Ten seconds and she's all yours.

"Doctor Crawford will be visiting before breakfast tomorrow and he won't be happy if you haven't slept a wink."

Tomorrow?

Tomorrow – but I'll be there.

Pull up blanket.

S'alright, Liza, she's drawing away.

Fingers numb, pickin at the paint.

Hush now, door locked. And dint I look after you?

Tomorrow morning, she said. The Crow…

It'll go soon as it's come, Liza. Nothing to worry about when I'm here. 'Member the creatures down Plumstead Road? Ever you were glum on the streets you'd think of them girls and their poor stories. 'Member Florence Collins? Met her your first time in the drum, and Christ was she miserable. Almost as wretched as you when –

Wunt shut up weeping, in for *mistreatment of child* because she shoved a carving fork right up there to kill it off. Silly girl only stabbed herself and when the butler saw a trail of splats, that was her, caught red-handed. Whether it belonged to the master or flue-faker she wunt say, but whoever it was they left her good 'n plump.

And second time you saw her, she was miserable too. But not bad as you when –

Carried into gaol with babber screaming in her arms. Caught nabbing bread. Nobody wants to hire a maid with an extra mouth to feed.

Not half as bad as Hetty Heigh, rotting with the glim. Dint even have a nose, last you saw her, Liza. And Hannah Rust –

Barely twelve when she burnt a house to a crisp. Master'd took his way with her and when no one listened to the servant girl, she sent him to Hell herself.

Int to mention the wicked ones.

Louise Cushion, pushing pins into children's bodies because she relished their screams. Sarah Makins, governess – arsenic in the afternoon tea.

And see, you dint ever do nothing like that. You wunt hurt a pidgeon, Liza – only us…

But they took me all the same. Seven times – in, out, in, out. Prison, court, docs, street.

What was your crime? *Lodging in the open. Wandering. Vagrancy.* You dint deserve a punishment for what you couldn't help.

Seven times.

(thck)

Smells like piss, smells like piss. Dunt these stones always smell like piss, Liza?

They say in the pad there's a gutter what runs round the floor, so when they lock you in you can spend a penny right there on the leather-pad walls.

How many nights have you slept on the stones?

Too many to count.

Kicked out of Providence Place afore you could sing God Save the Queen. Held our head high, Liza –

But none of the Johns'd have me.

Not for all the weeping in Norwich town. Found a shop door you could huddle, but then men were hauling you up by the arms –

Flung me like a doll. Rum on their breath as they pulled at my skirts – woke next morning in a pool of red. Paper hawker nudging me with his foot to see if pockets jangled. Could remember the rum, could remember the leering, not much beyond.

If it wunt July, we'd be dead afore sunrise, wouldn't we, Liza?

All because Ma spent my pennies on bottles. Should've paid the landlady myself. Should've known Ma'd drink it away.

That bitch.

Pushing me out to make gentlemen pay. All those fumbling fingers. Dirty, and you could feel the dirt, even when they were covered in fancy gloves and wiped with white kerchiefs. You were there, Anguish, but it was me what felt their fingers. Groping up my legs. Grunts in my ear. Sticky thighs and scratches on my back where they pushed me 'gainst the bricks.

But I hushed you –

Because I couldn't get the shiver out my bones, nor the bruises up my thighs. Little fingers. Fancy, fiddling fingers. Dark grey and round, bruises barely fading to yellow afore the next gentleman made his mark.

But I kept you company –

Couldn't keep me warm, could you, Anguish?

'Member the stories I would tell you, huddled down alleys? Picking at the bricks –

Least the Norwich streets had lanterns sparkling on wet cobbles – people chattering and noise of clattering. In here, just deep, cold lonely…

Come now, 'member –

What if I dunt want to remember? Farthing, farth –

Shutting me up?

– ha'penny –

Why? When I sang you to sleep every night, Liza. And found you shelter, food. I was there when you were out in the cold and I found you money, hushing you when they touched and when they raised their hands to beat us –

Me. They beat me.

– I stroked your hair and hushed you and I was there when you were crying in the corner… How long since you spoke to another person, Eliza?

(thck)

(thck)

How long? Weren't in here. Weren't in docs. Weren't in court.

So?

Pathetic.

And what does that make you, Anguish?

Dunt know, Eliza, you tell me.

– I made you up out of bits and bobs of nothing.

Pathetic.

Nothing.

Why the rope, Liza?

Farthing, farthing, ha'penny, two. One pence, tuppence…

TOMORROW

(thck)

(thck)

Outlines of beds looming grey. But if I shut my eyes and stroke my wall, I can see long ridges like river waves. Hollow, where the tip of my pinkie buries, snug. One hole here, and one crack like slicing meat pie. Straight and clean – criss-crossing rope burns – and morning. Soon. Count the pennies and she'll come. Farthing, farthing, ha'penny, two. One pence, tuppence, thrup'ny bit, groat.

(thck)

Anguish?

Nothing, am I, Eliza?

Dint mean –

You dint?

(thck)

Never mind, Eliza. Are you ready?

Corridor clacking…

Two paces unmatched. Hold the wall, lean back.

Anguish –

Jangle of her keys –

Anguish? I'm sorry.

Hush now, baby, Anguish'll take good care of you.

Crow.

'Matron tells me you were sitting here all night.'

Closer and closer – leather-black shoes, grey cloak, grey suit, grey tie, sparkling fobwatch and questions on the tip of his tongue…

Doctor, Doctor, I'm right at death's door. Don't worry, dear, we'll soon pull you through.

Not now, Anguish. Int funny.

Dunt you want me to help, Liza?

"This is perhaps a form of self-flagellation, wouldn't you say, Matron?"

"Oh yes, Doctor Crawford."

Why so close? If Crow touches… Anguish – keep me company, keep me safe.

"Well, Miss Bailey, do you think you might provide some answers today? I hear you spend your time in this corner, refusing to partake in any needlework or laundry. Is this true?"

Crouches down, takes hand out of pocket and draws finger cross my cheek, tilts my chin. Anguish? Keep me company…

"The devil makes work for idle hands."

"Indeed, Matron."

(thck)

"The only thing she ever does is hit the wall, pick the paint. I tell her not to, Doctor Crawford. Lack of respect –"

"I see. Very interesting. Can you tell me why you hit the wall, Miss Bailey?"

(thck)

"You won't get a word out of her, Doctor Crawford."

"Yet I shall continue, nevertheless. Perhaps, in the least, my questioning will prompt self-reflection."

Keep me safe...

"As you wish, Doctor Crawford."

Farthing, farthing, ha'penny...

"And you say she picks the paint?"

"That patch was all her. You can see the flakes around her feet, Doctor Crawford. I forbid it, but then –"

"I am sure you do, Matron. Miss Bailey, why do you pick at this wall?"

Anguish? Did I count you out or in? Keep me safe, Anguish.

'Do you think that perhaps you enjoy the destruction of the ward?'

Crow filling up my head. Farthing, farthing...

"Or perhaps, Miss Bailey, you are marking out territory?"

...thrupn'y bit, groat.

"Perhaps this is a form of communication?"

Anguish?

(thck)

"The slapping once more! Why is it you slap the wall, Miss Bailey?"

Anguish, I counted.

"An expression of frustration, perhaps?"

Anguish?

"Or, once more, communication?"

Anguish? Farthing, farthing...

"One avenue I would like to pursue, Matron, is another phrenological examination."

"The craniometer, Doctor Crawford?"

Anguish, please...

"Indeed, but I would rather conduct the examination in my office, Matron. If you could make a note to bring Miss Bailey tomorrow morning?"

"As you wish, Doctor Crawford."

Tomorrow morning, Anguish. The leather clamp, the craniometer, Anguish. Farthing, farthing...

"And tomorrow, Miss Bailey, you will need to prepare yourself for further questioning. As you must be aware, self-murder is a crime; it is a sin and thus, you must ask yourself why you chose this course of action. Why did you decide upon the rope?"

(thck)

(thck)

"Now, Matron, I believe it is time for Miss Bailey to reflect. Let us proceed to Ward Four…"

(thck)

'Member the first time you met Crow, Liza? Shook his head as he lifted your skirts. Shook his head at the marks round our neck…

Where were you, Anguish?

And that metal bit – got us all sudden and we shook, dint we, Liza?

I needed you, Anguish.

Not now, Anguish. Int funny.

I needed you.

Couldn't keep me warm, could you, Anguish?

But I needed you.

And what does that make you, Anguish?

You know that int what…

Nothing. Bits and bobs of nothing.

Dint mean –

Oh, but you did. Shutting me up, when I'm keeping you safe, keeping you company.

(thck)

Know what I think, Liza?

(thck)

That you're the one who's nothing. Done –

Dunt think you're nothing, Anguish.

– buggered without me.

You're keeping me safe, keeping company…

Say that to me now and shut me up later. Tell me, Liza. *Why did you decide upon the rope?*

Not now, Anguish.

Dunt trust me more than you trust Crow, do you, Liza?

Anguish, I'll count again. See if I dunt…

Why did you decide upon the rope?

Dunt say I dint warn –

But *why did you decide upon the rope? The Lord knows, Eliza Bailey, the Lord knows – think you're so clever, don't you?*

Farthing, farthing, ha'penny, two. One pence, tuppence, thrup'ny bit –

Doctor, doctor, I'm right at death's door. What's your name? What you done? Why you here?

Count the pennies. Count. Farthing, farthing, ha'penny –

Who do you bloody well think you are?

– ha'penny, two. One pence, tuppence –

My face is my fortune, sir, she said. Just a nibble, sir. Penny a nibble, sir.

Penny. Penny –

Penny a nibble, sir?

Penny nibble farthing farthing

What's your name? What you done? Why you here?

(thck)

Who are you?

(thck)

(thck)

Whoareyou?WhoareyouWhoareyou*whoareyouwhoareyouwhoareyouwhoareyou*

The Professor

– Anna Metcalfe –

At around two o'clock in the morning, smoke twisted its way into Ruth's dream so that her sister's face, which had been floating in and out of focus, clouded over. There was the sound of coughing and Ruth was trying to speak, to ask Helen if she was all right, when she woke up and understood that the coughing she had heard was, in fact, her own. The dream vanished and Ruth ran to the bedroom window and saw that the apartment block on the other side of the street was ablaze. Clouds of dark smoke rose up from it, the glow of the fire still bright within. Behind frames of shattered glass, large wooden beams glimmered and fell and ceilings appeared to melt. Ruth blinked. She thought about opening the window but didn't.

There was a knock at the door. Ruth ran to answer it and a fireman requested that she vacate her apartment.

It was the end of November and already near freezing. Ruth pulled her coat from the row of hooks in the narrow hallway. She only just remembered to pocket her key before following the fireman out onto the landing. She pointed at the professor's door, which stood directly opposite, and the fireman told her that the old lady was already outside.

At the third floor, the fireman said:

'Lucky it was no longer lived in.'

Ruth did not know how long he had been talking to her. She learned that, though the fire had been ferocious, they had managed to control it and it hadn't spread to any of the adjoining buildings, but that the whole street was being evacuated on account of the dangerous smoke.

'How did it happen?' said Ruth, as they reached the ground floor.

'I just told you,' said the fireman, ushering her towards the large group of evacuees. He went to join his colleagues at the gates of the burning building.

Ruth was taken to the designated safety area a couple of blocks down the road. She was given a blanket and offered tea in a paper cup which she refused. From here, she could still see the roof on fire. Looking up, there was a strange sensation of cold air and hot smoke against her face. Peals of orange light tore up the night sky. On the roof of one of the adjoining buildings, a little above the worst of the smoke, a row of firemen stood like toy soldiers on top of a child's wardrobe.

Residents spilled out into the street from all directions, a dishevelled, sleep-soaked muddle. Shaking off slumber and shuffling to safety, blankets wrapped around their pyjamas, they were regrouping into tight family circles or wider bands of friends. Among them were a few faces Ruth recognised, but there was no one she knew. She had only been living in the flat a couple of weeks. She was simply looking after it while her sister was away.

This was Ruth's first time living alone. Helen had gone travelling for three months just as Ruth was graduating and their parents suggested that Ruth take over the Brooklyn apartment and look for a job. It was a sensible move but Ruth had never been very good at making friends. It would have been one thing to move into a shared house but to move, just like that, with no job and no sister, was something for which she had not been entirely prepared. And now this: standing alone among a crowd of angry, anxious people, exhausted, Helen's face still following her, a hangover from the dream.

Ruth looked about and saw the professor who had placed herself a careful distance from everyone else. Unlike Ruth, she appeared to be perfectly content being alone, her arms folded in front of her and her body angled away from the crowd to indicate that she did not wish to be approached. The professor wore a long, tweed coat. Thick and clumsy-looking bed socks bunched over the sides of her heavy, brown boots. Ruth watched as she drew a pack of cigarettes from one pocket and a bright metal lighter from another. As she lit up, her eyes met Ruth's, just for a moment, and she nodded. Ruth nodded back but turned away, not wishing to intrude on the professor's solitude.

Since Ruth moved in, they had met on the shared landing several times, never exchanging more than a few simple words, though Ruth had always tried to initiate a conversation. As much as she was nervous, even shy, in the company of her peers, Ruth enjoyed the company of old people. It had never been a chore to her to visit her grandparents, as it had been for her other siblings. Ruth loved to listen to them talk and felt reassured by the solidity of their opinions. They knew what they liked. Others found this obstinate, but for Ruth it was a source of great comfort.

Ruth was offered another cup of tea, and this time she accepted. She drank half and let the rest go cold. Someone took the cup from her hands and replaced it with a fresh one. It was only when the fire had been reduced to smouldering ashes that they were allowed back to their end of the street and into their building.

When Ruth reached her sister's flat on the sixth floor, she found the professor lingering on the landing.

'Are you all right?' said Ruth. 'Do you have your key?'

'Yes,' said the professor. 'But I was wondering, would you come in for drink? I thought you might be shaken up.'

'Thank you,' said Ruth, 'Yes,' and she followed the professor through the door.

The professor's apartment was modestly decorated, the most elaborate item being an ornate writing desk by the window on which stood a large, pale-blue typewriter and three-tiered letter-holder that was laden with envelopes and postcards. The professor indicated that Ruth should sit in one of two, high-backed arm-chairs in the middle of the room. She walked over to the kitchen and returned with cut-glass tumblers, half-filled with an amber spirit. Ruth sniffed hers before sipping. Whisky. The smallest mouthful warmed her all the way through. The professor sat down in the other chair, holding her tumbler firmly in both hands. Ruth saw that her shoulders were trembling.

'Are you cold?' she said.

'A little,' said the professor. 'Perhaps you can fetch me a blanket from over there.' The professor pointed to a large chest on the far side of the room. Ruth put down her drink and went to get the blanket. She was surprised when the professor leant forwards to let Ruth drape it over her shoulders.

The professor was not talkative so they sat in silence, sipping their drinks. Ruth was taking it slowly but the professor drank quickly and soon got up to pour herself a second. When she sat down again she was holding a book. She held it out towards Ruth.

'Would you read it to me?' she said.

'Of course,' said Ruth and reached over to take the book from her hand.

Ruth looked at the book more closely: a slim volume, barely a novella, with a pretty orange cover and gold lettering.

She began to read. After the first ten pages, the professor closed her eyes and fell asleep. For a while, Ruth was not sure whether the professor was really asleep, or just dozing, so she carried on until she was approximately halfway through.

Before leaving, Ruth took the second blanket and spread it over the professor, tucking it in gently behind her knees as she had done when her grandparents were very old. She let herself out, making sure that the latch was down. It was not until she was back in her own apartment that Ruth realised she'd brought the book with her.

Invigorated by the events of the night, Ruth found that she was not in the least inclined to sleep so she sat up in bed and read to the end of the book. It was a strange and winding tale, foreboding and ominous. Ruth felt sure that the story would end badly, so sure in fact, that when she reached the last page she was surprised, heartened even, to find that everything turned out quite well. She could not explain why but the fact that the book had such a pleasing ending only increased her fondness for the professor.

In the morning, she knocked on the professor's door but there was no answer. Ruth went back to her flat and made a cup of coffee. Half an hour later, she tried again, but there was still no reply. She decided she would slip a note under the door.

She took some nice paper and a black pen from Helen's desk and in the neatest handwriting she could manage —she had a sense that the professor would appreciate neatness — she wrote a note informing the professor that the little book was safe in her possession and that she would keep it until such a time as might be convenient for the professor to pick it up. She slipped the note under the door and went on with the day.

Weeks passed and the professor made no response. Ruth got into the habit of listening for the professor's footsteps on the landing but she never managed to catch her going in or out. From time to time, Ruth would hear the shuffling of furniture or the clatter of crockery coming from the apartment. On these occasions, she would scuttle across and knock on the professor's door, but there was never any answer.

When Helen returned, Ruth told her about the fire and the professor and the book but she could not quite describe the need she felt to see the professor once again, to return the book in person. As Ruth packed up her things, several times she placed the little orange book in her satchel, along with the other books she had brought, but each time she took it out again, placing it somewhere obvious so that she would remember to ask Helen to give it back.

Carrying her luggage out onto the landing, Ruth kept hoping that the professor would be roused by the noise and open her door, but nothing happened. Ruth and Helen carried her belongings down to the taxi that was waiting outside. Helen stepped forward to give Ruth a cuddle, when Ruth said:

'I think I've forgotten something.'

Helen handed her the key and Ruth ran back inside. At the professor's door, Ruth stood and knocked for the very last time. She was sure that she heard footsteps inside but there was no answer and Ruth was left to wonder what it was that she had done that was had been so very wrong.

A Solitary For Two

– Ceridwen Edwards –

Not many people in Britain know what Buddhism is. I didn't either when I first started to meditate. But slowly over a few months I began to learn something of what it was and thought I might in fact be a Buddhist or at least was on the way to becoming one. And so I decided to test my practice and go on a solitary retreat.

My first solitary was for three days, in a cottage in Dunwich, near the edge of a cliff. During that time I learnt a few important things. That meditation is often the last thing I want to do. That I seem to have a lot of thoughts. And that it isn't a good idea to invite one's parents to tea on the last day of a solitary, however short it has been. Useful lessons that I resolved to remember.

My second solitary would be longer, I decided. However, I had heard of people coming back from three-week solitaries with stories of running out of food and seeing things. One person imagined a wolf prowling around the garden and another convinced herself she was going into a diabetic coma and phoned 999 only to be winched out of the place by mountain rescue helicopter. Such stories scared me. I had a good idea of what my mind was capable of and so decided I wouldn't spend more than a fortnight on my own.

I started telling my new Buddhist friends about this plan and to my surprise one of them, Teeny, said she was thinking of doing the same. She suggested we found a large enough place and went together.

'It would be cheaper and I could keep you out of the pubs.'

That was the kind of thing she said and was one of the reasons I hesitated. What decided me was remembering how important compassion is to a Buddhist. I would have plenty of opportunity to develop this, I reasoned, if Teeny came too. And after all, I had a lot to thank her for. She had helped me get to a Buddhist centre in the first place.

Four months earlier, I'd attended an assertiveness course and had been encouraged to take greater risks in my life. So, cycling home, I was on the lookout for something I could do that was a bit out of the ordinary. There was a small park I usually went through, keeping to the cycle track but this time I thought I'd go on the grass, zigzagging between the trees. It was getting dark when suddenly there was an intense pressure in my jaw and I found myself lying on the ground. A branch had got in my way. When I reached home, I was feeling pretty nauseous so I phoned NHS Direct who sent round a couple of paramedics to assess me. I opened the door to a very tall woman and a much smaller man.

'Frank Edwards?' the woman asked.

'Yes,' I said.

'Funny name for a woman?' commented the man.

'It's Franc,' I said, 'Like the old French money. Short for Frances.'

'Well, I'm not one to talk.' The woman bent slightly as she came through the door.

'Why? What's your name?'

She looked down at me. 'Teeny.'

'Really? Not a nickname?'

'No. I was over two foot long when I came out.'

'Parents with a sense of humour,' I said.

She ignored this. Perhaps I'd gone too far.

'You're very good at this,' I told her, remembering the risk-taking advice. She *was* good too, calm and reassuring.

'Do you think so?' She looked pleased, 'Thanks. I've only been doing it for a few weeks. He's learning me the ropes.'

I wasn't sure if that was deliberate. She had a very educated accent bordering on the posh.

'Yes, you seem very together and unfazed.'

'That'll be the meditation. I just started a course this week. It's not easy but I'm getting a lot out of it.'

I saw this as a sign. I'd wanted to learn to meditate for ages but had never got round to it. The following week I went along to the Cambridge Buddhist centre and joined the same meditation course as Teeny.

As we got to know each other it became clear that we were very different characters. I loved the idea of renunciation and immediately put it into practice, giving away most of my furniture, books and kitchen equipment with the idea of living a more simple, uncluttered life. Teeny hadn't been at all keen to join me in my newfound enthusiasm. I soon found out why.

She lived, I discovered, in a large house in north Cambridge, each wall downstairs filled from floor to ceiling with deep shelves crammed with objects. Books, loose papers, files, old china plates and teapots, empty candlesticks, stuffed birds in belljars, African baskets and more. Everything seemed precariously balanced and in complete disorder. The walls were covered with framed prints of Victorian-looking Jesuses and scenes of a biblical nature. Then was the furniture - cupboards, dressers, sofas, trunks, chests, armchairs and tables – built up into great piles in the middle of each room like a village bonfire or an art installation, with only a narrow space round the edges. It was a weird sight. I was shocked that she could live like this.

'Why so many things, Teeny? Think of the Buddha. One robe, one bowl.'

'Oh, please don't have a bloody go at me.'

This was another difference between us. Her language.

'But why do you need all this? It's too much for one person. I could help you sort through it.'

It was then that she told me more about her past. Her parents had both died ten years before, when she'd been at university in York. They'd been missionaries in Burkina Faso and had caught some water-borne tropical disease, which had killed them both in a week.

Teeny, an only child, had immediately returned to their family home in Cambridge She had piled up the downstairs furniture in her frantic grief and lived in the small spaces that remained. The front room represented her father and the back room, her mother. She seemed to have no interest in changing the situation. I was one of a few people, apart from a couple of boyfriends, she had ever invited inside the house. Upstairs the bedrooms were normal.

'I feel safe in there,' she told me pointing to a narrow entrance into the 'father' pile. 'All these bits of furniture remind me of Dad and make me feel he's still here with me.'

I was beginning to see our time away together might not be as simple as I had originally thought it would be.

We decided to go to a place we had heard of in North Wales, near Port Madoc. Other people had been there and said it was remote and had a view over a tidal bay. It was a three-room shack with a primitive outside loo/bathroom, a large room downstairs, including a cooking area, and two small bedrooms above. It sounded perfect. Teeny wasn't so keen.

'Are you sure it's got running water? How will we get food? Are the mattresses ok?'

She had question after question.

'Look,' I said, 'If you don't want to go, that's fine. It's cheap enough for me to go on my own.'

I was really looking forward to some time away, with or without Teeny. I decided to travel as light as I could, taking only one book, Nanamoli's 'Life of the Buddha', which I planned to annotate, a couple of changes of clothing, cagoul and a minimal amount of wash gear, walking boots and my meditation stool. That was about it.

On the morning of departure, there was a Teeny kind of sandwich at the station as she stood propped between two huge rucksacks. I decided not to say anything after having seen her house. As the Dalai Lama says, 'Kindness is my practice.'

It was a long journey. By the time we reached Minffordd I'd got a good way through my book and was wishing I'd brought more. Teeny refused to tell me how many books she'd packed. She sat reading 'The Hitch-Hiker's Guide to the Galaxy' throughout the journey, snorting with laughter and often glancing at me. I could tell she wanted to read bits out loud and was glad I'd insisted our journey be in silence. I wanted the travelling to be part of the retreat. As I looked out at the Welsh mountains, I chanted mantras under my breath. I felt so alive to my experience.

We had agreed to talk as we walked around the Port Madoc Tesco's. I began to regret it though as we had such different ideas about what to eat on a retreat.

'Oh come on,' laughed Teeny, 'I'm not living off lentils and beans for two weeks! And you won't want me too either once you hear what they do to me. We need *some* treats.'

I gave in finally, as she wouldn't stop going on about it, and we put in a few packets of Quorn burgers and even two avocados. But I drew the line at puddings. If it had been up to Teeny, the whole trolley would have consisted of yoghurts and biscuits.

By the time we'd caught a taxi to the retreat place, it was dark and we couldn't see much of our surroundings. The shack was hard to find as it was hidden in trees, away from the road, down a steep slope through woods. Both of us had forgotten torches but Teeny had brought her phone, despite my advice, so our path was lit by twenty-first century technology. It wasn't the mythical way I had imagined arriving.

The hut was basic. Even I was a bit discouraged at the sight of the interior. There was no wood or dried kindling for the wood-burner and the place was chilly and damp. The weather forecast that day said autumn had arrived. Teeny went up the wooden ladder carefully to check out the bedrooms. Her face peered down at me.

'Do you want the good news or the bad?' She looked serious.

'Bad, always first.'

'One mattress is wringing wet. It's actually dripping onto the floor. I think it must be under a leak.'

'And the good?'

'The other one's only damp. Though it's covered in what I think are mice droppings…or rats.'

All the bedding was soaking too and there were no spare, dry blankets.

We spent that night sitting upright in chairs, each wearing items from Teeny's copious retreat wardrobe. She'd brought four jumpers, several large woollen shawls, pairs of thick walking socks and a couple of felt hats. We looked ridiculous but were at least warm. However, I got little sleep. Teeny had the steady snore of a carpenter's saw which kept going and going despite my sharp coughs and repeatedly throwing my hat at her. I tried to use the time to meditate but the rhythmic sound ground through every good intention. By dawn, I was wondering whether putting a plastic bag over her head would stop her. Welsh rain poured down the window as if from a jug .

Finally, around seven o'clock she gave an extra loud snort and woke up. She groaned.

'God, that was a dreadful night. I'm so stiff!'

I took a deep breath. 'Well, I'm glad you got some sleep. I had to sit here listening to you all night.'

'Really? Do I talk in my sleep? What did I say?'

It was hard to believe she didn't know she snored though it turned out all her ex-boyfriends had been avid snorers themselves. At least she knew how I felt. She offered to make breakfast.

It took another day of solid rain before we decided to go home.

I'm always learning things through my Buddhist practice even from that brief time away in Wales. In this case, I think it was that we are not who we think we are. We are deluded. Teeny and I are still good friends.

The Bridge

– Caitlin Ingham –

We hadn't been to America since my grandmother had died ten years before. I think there might have been an argument at the time, something about who to invite to her funeral or who got her flat perhaps. Whenever I had asked my mother to describe the cause of the rift, she'd been evasive; 'I'll tell you when you're older' or 'Oh it's all so tiresome.' Her reluctance to explain made me think she hadn't been completely innocent in the affair herself, but I had never pressed it with her. In any case, the various branches of the family hadn't met for years, but our eleven-hour and vastly expensive flights from England meant that all the relatives had no choice but to travel from their different corners of the States. And there it was - a family reunion.

A walk had been arranged for the second day, earnestly referred to as a 'hike' by all the aunts and uncles, despite the fact it was taking place in a botanical garden. My brother was soon surrounded by aunties, laughing and praising, so I made a beeline for the only relative younger than me - my cousin Esther. I barely knew her; to me she was defined by an early memory I had of her spraying a pet parrot with window cleaner until all its feathers fell out. She had since grown into an almost-teenager and was wearing an enormous sweatshirt with black leggings that emphasised her impossibly scrawny legs. It was only in noticing quite how skinny and small she was and in thinking how unusual the combination was among the women in my mother's family that the memory resurfaced: Esther was adopted.

I felt terrible for having forgotten this upsetting episode of family history. I recalled how my aunt had discovered she couldn't get pregnant, and the torturous process she went through with my uncle before finally succeeding in taking home a baby girl from an orphanage in Romania. I suppose I had only been a little kid myself at the time.

'Hi Esther. You remember me?' I said.

She gave me a brief but pretty smile. I asked her everything I could think of - how old she was, whether she still had a parrot, what kind of music she liked. Her answers were polite but mostly monosyllabic. Eventually all I could think to say was 'Gosh, I love your accent.'

She looked up and asked, 'Why? I don't have an accent.'

We walked together, passively watching the animated conversations of the adults before us. After perhaps half a mile of manicured bushes and pointy flowers, the path relaxed a bit and turned into a small forest. Esther and I seemed to wordlessly agree to break off from the family procession and walk through it. Strewn twigs and thick, mossy trunks made it seem as if we'd discovered some genuine, wild nature, until I saw a clearing through the leaves and stuck up in the earth were two quaint little STOP and GO signs. There we spotted a miniature train track creeping over the forest floor. For a moment we both examined it seriously; the track was obviously in use but only a couple of feet wide - the train it hosted couldn't have been higher than my shoulders.

I turned to Esther. 'Pretty cool isn't it?'

She ignored me and peered around, looking for the train to come. Then she squatted and started to gather the small rocks around the tracks. She picked up dozens of fist-sized stones, eventually using her jumper as a makeshift net to hold them in. She scrabbled around for several minutes, showing no sign of stopping.

'Esther, what are you doing?' I asked.

She didn't answer. Exasperated, I decided to leave her to it, stepping carefully back through the trees. When I was a short distance away, I turned around to check if she'd stopped and saw that she'd actually started to pile a mound of rocks onto the train track.

'What the *fuck* are you doing?' I screamed, running to her.

She didn't look up and continued to stack the stones on the tracks, selecting edges that fit together like jigsaw pieces to secure them. Her movements were as confident and decisive as a skilled workman.

'Esther, are you trying to derail the train?'

She smiled. 'Yeah,' she said, 'it'll be funny.'

I stared at her in disbelief. Then, hearing a mechanical sound from down the tracks, looked up and saw the train approaching, about fifty metres away. There were at least twenty children crammed on its miniature carriages. Esther acted with intense concentration, building the stones up even faster, piling up a sturdy dam. I had no idea how the physics of this scenario would unfold and whether the rocks would cause the entire train to derail, and was rapidly gripped by panic. I grabbed Esther hard by her puny shoulders and threw her to the side, while at the same time trying to kick out the stones. She had amassed a surprisingly hefty pile. I frantically kicked and scooped, watching the train move closer and closer, the driver now standing up and staring in alarm. Esther was slumped on the ground, crying angrily; one of the rocks I'd thrown had hit her I think. She jumped up and whacked me on my back, but I ignored her, focussing on pulling out the last of the stones. I actually managed to clear the track completely; the train still several metres away. I sat panting on the ground and watched it chug by, the driver gawping down at us whilst the line of kids waved, oblivious in their excitement.

Esther and I walked back together in wounded silence.

Eventually I spoke, 'I'm sorry if I hit you. Why were you doing that though? You could have really hurt those kids.'

She didn't respond. When we neared the group, she ran ahead until she was a few metres behind her mother, who she followed, silent and unnoticed.

The week passed, time marked by one enormous meal after another. Stilted chat turned into real, weighty conversations and slowly people came to know each other again. My mother was giddy; she referred to a grilled cheese sandwich as 'poignant' at one point and I quite often caught her staring tenderly at my brother and me. But despite all of the successes, the relentless schedule of interactions eventually gave rise to snubs and quibbles and building tension. Soon the mood between the adults started to wilt. I suspected that Esther had been avoiding me. She was solitary in general but the distance between the two of us had become marked. On the last day of the trip there was a plan to take a boat out to a restaurant in a bay area outside the city.

We sat around plastic tables on seats that were glued to the floor. My brother laid his head against our mother's chest while she stroked it and played with his hair. His twenty-year-old, stubbly face made the action look gross; he wouldn't have dreamed of displaying such babyish affection a week ago, but family holidays seemed to make people odd and at this point he looked near to sucking his thumb.

I felt a tap on my shoulder and turned to see Esther, her face turned up towards me, pale and expectant.

'What's up?' I said, hiding my surprise.

'Come to the bathroom with me.'

'Why?'

She didn't answer, just walked away, a quick shake of her hand suggesting I should follow her. There was only one toilet cubicle, which was tiny, but Esther pulled me in.

'Don't tell anyone.'

'What?'

'I've got blood in my underwear.' She tried to sound as if it were a minor annoyance but her voice dripped with fear.

'Oh. You know what that will be?'

'Period.'

The word seemed to bounce of the walls of the cubicle and embarrass us both.

'Yes, it probably will be. Is this your first one?'

'Yes.'

'Congratulations!' I said, purely because that is what my mother said to me. 'Don't you think you should tell your mum?'

'No. She will tell everyone, she'll tell Dad, then your mom and Aunt Sally and they'll all talk about it all day.'

She was exactly right, of course. I felt bad not to have thought of that myself.

'Ok. Has it gone on your clothes?'

'No. Not yet.'

'Ok, I can sort this, I'll be back in a second.'

I started to unlock the bathroom door, she grabbed me and hissed, 'Don't tell anyone!'

'I won't! I promise.'

I returned to the table, considering my options. My brother's head now lay as the lazy centrepiece of the table, my mother talking to my aunts while still scratching his hair in the languid fashion a lioness might groom her cub. I picked up her handbag.

'What do you want?' she asked.

'Gum.' She reached into her pocket so I said, 'Oh I need money too. For a coke.' She rolled her eyes and turned her attention back to her conversation and I managed to grab a couple of tampons and slip them into my pocket without her noticing.

I went back to the bathroom and knocked on the door. Esther didn't open it until she heard my voice. Her face was red and glistening, from what I realised were quickly rubbed-in tears. Her demeanour was defiantly void of emotion, but the wet and ruddy cheeks betrayed her. I thought of the way she must have allowed herself to cry alone in the toilet just for the minute I was gone and felt a sudden surge of compassion.

I passed her the stuff, 'Do you know what to do?'

She affirmed grimly, 'I just watched a tutorial on my phone.'

'Good. I'll wait outside the bathroom, OK?'

I did, hearing angry shuffling around and the occasional humph of frustration. Eventually she came out and we nodded at each other, hard and silent like gang members after a hit. We immediately went back to sitting with our own families - Esther clearly flustered and self-conscious. I was too.

Everyone dozed and I became restless. There was a staircase in the corner, which looked off limits but lacked any sort of notice explicitly saying so. I started to climb, the brightness increasing with every step I took. I realised I going up to the open-air deck but the vigorous wind and strength of light was still a beautiful shock. The sky was a ludicrous pale blue, the kind of fake colour that you normally only see painted on eggshells or on baby-boy clothes. The water was much darker, and tacky with diamonds. And then as if these great, bragging expanses of blue weren't enough, smack in the middle was the burnt orange of the Golden Gate Bridge, cutting the sky with staggering curves and a web of elaborate supports. It was almost obscene, the clamour of beauty. I couldn't believe that everyone was below the deck snoozing on the crappy furniture under the grim lighting and missing this. It was hard to tell if the bridge was supported from the base or held up by the gigantic suspensions. Did each cable actually play a part in keeping that thing up? There were at least four lanes of traffic zooming over and the headlights whizzed by relentlessly.

I heard some steps clanging up the staircase and turned around to see Esther.

'Hello.'

'Hey.'

'Oh!' she exclaimed quite suddenly, as if something had jolted her memory. 'You know I was only kidding. In the park I mean. I was going to take the rocks off before the train came; I just thought it would be funny to make you think I was doing that. Me and my friends play that game there all the time.' She smiled at me, with a convincing cheekiness, although I was still not sure I believed her.

'Ok,' I said. 'Well, you definitely got me!'

'My mom is arguing with your mom downstairs,' she then said. 'I don't see why they don't just come up here and look at the view - it's really nice right?'

We stood together, as the boat ploughed under Golden Gate Bridge, in a family sort of silence.

For Dave Garner

– Bethany Settle –

This began from a dream.

In it, Mr Garner and I meet again after a decade – we're running a poetry workshop for eight year olds, alongside other 'mentors'. He looks glowy, absurdly healthy, his face less wrinkled than I remember. We talk nonstop for ten minutes, then realise our kids have organised themselves and started without us. Sheepishly we turn to the task in hand, promising to speak again soon - he says maybe he'll visit me at my house in Norwich, I say that'll be lovely: then we can have a proper, in-depth catch-up.

On waking I felt pleased to have seen him. It brought back good memories and I wished I really could catch up with him. Then I thought he might be dead, that perhaps my dream had been one of those dreams I'd read about, where the dead went round looking radiant, tying up loose ends and visiting people whom they were important to, summoned by the invisible force of connection.

A hardworking and intelligent student who has blossomed

Mr Garner was my teacher in Sixth Form for both Media Studies and Drama. I'd left the Girls Grammar School in the next town where I'd felt limited, a middling student of academic subjects, and had joined the comprehensive down the road, where I already had a few friends. I thrived in the new environment and on my choice of creative subjects. Somewhere along the way I shaved my head.

I loved Mr Garner straight away. He was northern and gruff, with big wide ideas, and higher expectations of us than we had. He waved his arms around all the time, fingers spread at angles like the wing feathers of a crow, shouting new conceptual words at us in passion. Ideology! Hegemony! Paradigmatic!

He had a grey ponytail and an earring, always wore Doc Martens and walked with his hands stuffed in his pockets like he'd thrust them in with some violence. His battered, bright yellow VW van stood out amongst the silver family cars in the staff car park. He smelled always of fags. Once, when a small group of us had to attend an extra lesson during the holidays, he opened all the windows of his mobile classroom and let the smokers light up. He was anarchic and unusual, frank and clever. I was intrigued by the dynamics between him and the other teachers: did he stand alone or was he part of a team? Certainly he wasn't trying to fit in. That's one of the reasons I loved him. He wasn't afraid to be himself.

In lessons sometimes I'd get fixated on his expressive hands as he continually gestured. I'd never seen hands like them: big and coarse with a unique, awkward grace. I wrote a tiny story about how my hands were transforming into Mr Garner's, no one noticing except for me.

Thanks for your enthusiasm and erudition which made it all worthwhile

I loved Mr Garner, yes. I wasn't obsessed with him though, and I don't *think* I fancied him. Really, I loved everything about Sixth Form. We were a small band of students, there by choice, so everyone was friendly. And the teachers treated you like individuals instead of forcing you into little rule-holes. In Sixth Form I found a joyous balance between feeling engaged and being encouraged, and for the first time ever I actually enjoyed working hard.

Lots of teachers found me a pleasure to teach - they said so in my school reports. I was enthusiastic, ate knowledge like sweets. My boundaries were exploding and I was hungry for art, culture, ideas. Although I dressed 'individually', often badly in comparison to my fellow students, I was sweet and wanted to be kind to everyone. After a year I was elected Head Girl, which was incredible to me.

Just enjoy everything

I'd long realised that university was my way out to the wider world but was unsure what to study. Mr Garner suggested creative writing. I hadn't known you could study that. In a whoosh, all the writing I'd done since childhood, for fun or catharsis, coalesced into significance. I began to write more and in earnest. Mr Garner said I should apply to UEA as it had the best reputation. I went for an open day and didn't bother visiting any other universities after that. I'd fallen for the red autumn ivy hugging all that beautiful concrete, was desperate to live in a ziggurat with a lake view. When I was offered a place on the English with Creative Writing BA I was astounded.

I vowed that I would dedicate my first published novel to Dave Garner alone. There he was in my life's path like a sharp corner I'd turned, towards writing. The dedication would be simple in its gratitude: it would state how much I owed to him, and how big an influence he'd been during my most formative years. I've never regretted this vow - Mr Garner's suggestions set the course for my adult life.

But after my dream I thought, shit I still haven't written a novel: if he's dead he'll never know how much he meant to me and how much he changed my life.

Who am I going to live on now you've gone

We'd lost contact a long time ago. Probably my fault - uni was a compelling new world. But I also felt embarrassed by my depth of feeling for him, sure that if I insisted on keeping in touch (hoping we'd become actual friends), he'd think me weird. Students are supposed to grow up and move on: the teacher gets a fresh batch to develop and inspire. Some years ago however, Dave Garner turned up on Facebook and sent me a message saying hello. His profile picture was a black and white photo of him as a child riding a donkey. I replied to that message, but heard nothing back. The photo never changed and his page was never added to. I checked it periodically over the years, but no further activity.

Just remember me

That morning after the dream, I rolled over instinctively to check Facebook on my phone. His page was gone. No Dave Garner. I assumed Facebook had deleted his unused account but still its absence unsettled me. Maybe I'd lost him forever.

I kept on thinking about him all day. Memories and details resurfaced. His baby daughter had been obsessed with question marks. The time a few of us got to ride in his loud and juddery yellow van. When I went back to visit him during my first year of uni and we sat in the teachers' smoking lounge together, which turned out to be only a tiny cramped bit of the basement full of gigantic pipes.

At work, during the more routine tasks, I concocted a bizarre fictional situation that began with me finding his Facebook page after all. I sent a message about my dream. He didn't reply but I continued to send him messages anyway, for months, knowing they'd never be read. Of course, it culminated in him eventually reading every single one, and being quite freaked out by the peculiarity of it all.

It occurred to me - even if Mr Garner *was* dead, I could still try and communicate with him. Maybe he *would* visit me at my house in Norwich, appearing on my sofa one day, or materialising through the front door, and we would catch up like we'd agreed in the dream. Then it occurred to me that even if I felt no inkling of his presence, I could simply talk aloud to him hoping that he'd be listening.

I know you will go out there and be something

I found myself re-imagining my bizarre fictional situation as a piece of writing, where I would chat to his ghost in my front room for some months until one day I would run into him on a visit to my home county, walking down the road. Alive! His face would be more wrinkled, though it'd turn out he'd managed to quit the fags. We'd speak for a while and he'd say something inspiring, that would give me confidence for my future. On impulse I would hug him and, rather than freak out, he would be touched.

But I felt unsatisfied with this ending. I was a little disturbed by how neatly I'd wrapped it all up.

A better ending, I decided, needed to incorporate some truths. That the dream had left me feeling regretful that we'd lost touch but I was too timid to try contacting him through other teachers, old school-mates, or advertising in the local paper. That I wanted badly to commemorate him, to tell the world what a brilliant and truly important figure he was to me, but I didn't know if I'd ever actually bloody finish a novel to dedicate to him, let alone get it published. That I hadn't delivered on the promise and potential he and others saw in me back then. Mr Garner thought I would grow up to do something, to be somebody. I hadn't done much yet. I'd let lack of confidence and fear keep me quiet for far too long.

Is prepared to take risks in order to examine things in a different way

That night I ransacked boxes and cupboards, discovered journals and diaries, schoolwork, lists. A notebook of messages from friends and teachers on the last day of Sixth Form. Immersed, I forgot about starting dinner and putting a wash on. I didn't recognise myself. I couldn't remember being that person.

In some ways I hadn't been like other students. Aside from my colourful appearance and conspicuously keen attitude to learning (revision and homework to-do lists revealed I'd worked way harder than I could recall), I'd had a tattoo (when 16) and had dated a 31 year-old artist (at 17). I'd smoked, drank and had *loved* to swear - but hadn't done drugs or had sex (at all, until the artist). I'd been careful with my body, even post-virginity - apart from allowing my closest friend to photograph me topless in Klimt poses for her A-Level Art project (she hadn't been careful with the photos). People had often told me I had an old head on young shoulders.

Going through my diaries, I rediscovered that person. I seemed thrilling, exotic, far-reaching, determined.

Later, in bed, I thought about the book of personal essays that I'd finished reading the previous week, Ann Patchett's 'This Is the Story of a Happy Marriage'. I'd never read that sort of non-fiction before. I'd never tried to write that sort of non-fiction either. I decided to try something new for once.

Interesting and interested

Dave Garner was a new kind of adult to me. He was interesting, and interested. And when he wrote that about me in my school report, I took it deeply to heart. No adult had ever called me interesting. I'd collected 'vain', 'pretentious', 'weird' and 'macabre' off my Mum. But Mr Garner thought I had value as a person, and because of that I bloomed during that time. I'm determined to do so again.

I am already older than I ever imagined being when I was in Sixth Form. I don't have a glittering career, no, I haven't even written a novel yet - but. Recently I have begun to move away from thinking like that. It comes from vaguely formed ideas about success, self-expression and creativity that I have outgrown. Now I find I want authenticity, in as many different creative forms as possible.

I need to be a supportive, encouraging, interesting teacher to myself, allow myself to once more try my best, direct my focus, and work as hard as I did back then.

I have to be my own Dave Garner now. Although, if you're reading this Dave, *please* do come and visit me at my house in Norwich. Can we be friends?

Push

–Louise Ells –

Pushing. Pushing up through - thick green water, sludge, weeds, algae. Surfacing. Breathe, breathe. Focus.

Focus.

Her eyes are open. Aren't they?

'Here you are!' A young female voice.

Who's speaking? Where's here? There's no water. She tries to turn her head to make sense of her location, but can't twist her neck.

Opens her eyes wider. White plaster rose and chandelier. Her living room ceiling. Montreal.

'That was a bad one, but it's over now. Let's make you comfortable.'

Not comfortable. Everything hurts, a dull ache. A whirring sound and the chair jerks up, forcing her into what's called a sitting position. She tries to shift. Can't.

Blankets are tucked around her legs. 'There we go, Marie. Better now. And I have your meds. Would you like water or juice?'

Gabrielle. Giving her the illusion of choice. Two years ago, when she could still control her swallowing, that's when she should have refused medication and food. Too late now.

'Here's the pink one.'

The one that causes the hallucinations. Caught in a fire, buried alive, drowning in mud. Terrified, then always coming back to discover she's not dead. If she could make herself understood, she'd tell this girl she'd prefer the dyskinesia.

'And here's the blue one. And some more orange juice to help you swallow.'

But her head jerks at the wrong time. She feels liquid on her collarbone, a drop of it running from the soft cloth that wipes her mouth, her chin, her neck.

'Let's try that one again, shall we.'

The drugs. Anti-nausea, anti-indigestion, antidepressants. She can't feel her throat swallow the pills, but the taste of the reconstituted concentrate lingers on her tongue. A brief sense of her mother's hands on hers as they squeezed oranges for juice.

Do her hands look like her mother's did at the end, paper thin and tinged with blue? She tries to lift her right one.

'Your hands? I heard that very clearly.' A gentle touch. 'Ooh, icy cold. Here, I'll give them a rub to warm them up.'

Just as she used to rub her mother's hands and feet each morning. And every afternoon in the park she'd wrap her hands over her mother's around the thermos of hot chocolate as they watched the world. Her mother, when she could still speak, shared stories of harsh Maritime winters and thin boots stuffed with newspapers.

'Papers, was that? Would you like me to read you today's newspaper?'

No. But that word doesn't make it from her mind, through her throat and out into the room. Gabrielle has already gone in search of the newspaper, which she'll read cover to cover if she thinks that's what Marie desires. Kind, really. And it fills time.

She feels the drugs pulling her away from clarity.

Something she wanted to say.

Can't recall.

Her window of words, for today, is over.

Her eyes open. Dull, pre-dawn shadows. She's in the room they call her bedroom. Except it's not, not any more. Her sleigh bed with its soft mattress replaced by this narrow, hard hospital contraption. Her Edwardian side table displaced by the hoist. Her collection of vases bunched to one end of the mantelpiece to make room for rows of pill bottles.

Opens her eyes and watches light move across the wall. Late afternoon then, that's when this window catches the sun. Weekday or weekend? She listens for children on their way home from school and the start of rush hour traffic clogging up Westmount. Buses, horns. A jigsaw puzzle of sounds to piece together. And closer, two sets of footsteps.

'The rain's stopped and it looks lovely out there. Let's get you wrapped up and we'll go for a walk.'

Wrapped up. The carers' euphemism for the hour-long process to transfer her from bed to electric chair via hoist, wheel her into the wet room for a sponge bath and force her body into clothes. Then move her outside by way of a series of ramps. The bone-shakers, her mother had called them.

'I didn't catch that. Can you try again, please?'

She doesn't understand how it is that she has no idea when she's speaking aloud and no way to differentiate between words and nonsense sounds. The hoist swings her above the wheelchair and she sees the stain, notices one girl mouthing 'dry' to the other.

Her mother's wheelchair, stained with blood, sat in the front hall for three months after the police returned it. She left it where it was until the day she walked into it, couldn't catch herself in time, and fell over. Knew she was lucky not to have broken a hip. She put it out on the kerb by the trash and the next morning, long before the garbage men came, it was gone.

The girls take turns pushing her along the sidewalk towards Mount Royal. She knows this hill is hard work. They reach the pond and stop beside a bench, sit next to her and throw leftover cake to the ducks.

Just as she and her mother used to do, every afternoon. Isn't this nice, watching the world, she always said, trying to make it sound as if they were the lucky ones, the pair who could afford to sit and relax while everyone else rushed by. Once, her mother answered her. 'Not enough.' She'd heard her, but hadn't known what to do with the words.

A child runs past, stops and looks up at her, runs off again. 'Papa, Papa! Regardez-vous? Cette vieille dame est baver comme un bébé.'

Old. I'm sixty-three.

Gabrielle leans over and wipes the line of drool from her mouth. 'So many ducks,' she says. 'Look at that beautiful black and white one. I wonder what it's called.'

I was a partner in a law firm. My interests were antiques and gardening, never bird watching. Barrow's Goldeneye.

'Garrot d'Islande,' says the other carer at the same time. Followed immediately by, 'Sorry, I spoke over you. What is the name in English?'

But the two words won't come again.

So the carers talk about a movie they want to see, pretending the conversation includes her.

She isn't ungrateful. Lucky to be able to afford private care. In a home she'd be left in front of a television all day, no one would push her here every afternoon to feel the sun on her face.

'We'll stop for groceries at the dep on the way home, shall we? What do you fancy for dinner?'

- pasta fagioli. She discovered it on Sicily. That walking holiday with… she's lost his name. But the thick, rich soup, sweet with garlic and the seaside patio where they ate bowlful, after bowlful of it.

'Pâté? Sure.' Something that can be puréed, fed to her by teaspoon, but she can't make the word 'pasta' clear enough to be understood.

Banging on the front door. Now they're coming for her; she won't fight, she always knew they'd find her guilty. No sound then, no protest.

'Shh, shh, it's OK. You've just had one of those nasty hallucinations.'

Darkness. Disconcerting, this constant loss of time. Never knowing the hour or day or sometimes even the month.

'There aren't any police, you haven't murdered anyone.' It's not a voice she recognises. A new carer.

I'm sorry, I've forgotten your name.

'Emmeline, but everyone calls me Emmie.'

Emmie. Would you be so kind as to plump my pillow?

'Of course I will!'

Lovely. Thank you. And it truly is.

'A conversation, what a treat. I'll plump your pillow for you any time, and do anything else you ask. I wish I could always understand you this well.'

But it's plain from Emmie's face that the next words are just a jumble. The clear speech, an after-effect of the hallucination, has worn off. She wishes she could close her eyes and curl into her pillow.

Pillows. At some point it had stopped being a joke when her mother begged her to put a pillow over her face and it had ceased to scare her that she took her mother's requests seriously. But they had filled the evenings watching murder mysteries on television, and they both knew that murder by smothering left too many clues. A face imprint, skin cells.

Wakes to: 'Snow! Let's go to the park before it melts into a slushy mess.' She's being hoisted, put into a winter coat, hat and gloves. The girls hurry. She knows why; any change in routine is exciting.

It was the same when she was the caregiver. Guess who's come to visit you? She'd ask her mother in a voice, artificial even to her own ears. As if the community health nurse, Mathis, was worth the fuss of finger sandwiches and home-made butter tarts on fine china. But he was their only visitor for weeks at a time and generous enough to spend the extra half hour chatting over tea. It was Mathis who took her aside to ask her about her own health although she insisted the shaking was caused by stress, exhaustion. Even in denial she was just like her mother.

The park is full of children. 'A snow day,' says Emmie. 'First of the winter.'

'We never had this many snow days when I was at school,' says Gabrielle. She points. 'Look at them all, Marie. Tobogganing and snowmen. So much fun to watch, eh?'

Not enough.

No response. Have they not heard her or has she not spoken? Or do they, too, think it's best to let the words fade.

Church bells ring out. A wedding or a funeral? Or just the bell ringers practicing for Sunday's service?

I'd like to see Father Edwards, to make confession.

'Further inwards? In to the park?' Gabrielle is leaning close to Marie, searching her eyes for clues.

'It's rare that a mother and child are both struck with Parkinson's,' Mathis had said. 'We don't even know if there's a genetic link. But please, consider a check-up.'

So she'd gone. But when the results came back she couldn't share them with her mother. As best she could, she'd hidden the stumbling, imbalance, moments when she froze. She hid her own medication and looked away from her mother's gaze.

'We came out so early we nearly forgot your morning meds,' says Gabrielle. 'Look, Emmie's bought us some hot chocolate. With whipped cream no less.' She blows on it to cool it, then offers a tiny spoonful of cream with tablet. 'Here you go. Good. One more. And, last one.'

The last one. If only I could be sure it was.

'Have another sip. Isn't it lovely?'

Mother and I on this same bench, drinking hot chocolate. That day.

A small girl, blonde curls and bright pink snowsuit runs past, flops into the snow and waves her arms about. She jumps up, giggles at the shape she's left in the snow and dashes away.

'Shall we?' Emmie laughs. 'I wonder what people would say if the three of us lay down in the snow and started making angels.'

I'd like that.

'Would you?' Emmie turns to smile at her.

The drugs must have kicked in quickly. Her speech is strong and sure. This is her chance. Today, with the sun on the snow. Please, could push me up the Olmsted Trail?

'You want us to work off that hot chocolate and whipped cream, don't you?' Gabrielle says. 'Sure, it'll be a great view from the top. We'll be able to see all of Montreal and along the Saint Laurent.'

Emmie points to the sky. 'Look at those clouds moving in. More snow, I bet. I hope this means we'll have a good ski season.'

Hope. I live in hope.

'Oh. Marie.' Emmie looks at her. 'One day, you know. One day they'll find a cure for this shitty disease. God willing it will be in your lifetime.' She kneels to tuck the blankets around her. 'And I saw from your photo albums that you were a skier. Me and my big mouth, I'm sorry.'

Emmie has misunderstood. It's not a cure she's hoping for, or a day of skiing. Her chair's wheels slipping on the snow or a frozen patch on the shady sidewalk; a momentary loss of control.

A moment. That's all it was that day, between the holding of the handles and her mother's chair in the road, a car unable to swerve or stop.

That day.

Mathis had met her at the hospital, sat with her in the beige room when the doctors spoke to her, and again when the policewoman interviewed her. A tragic accident, Mathis said. Tragic, the policewoman agreed.

The medication is affecting her memory. She isn't sure. Was it just an icy patch? Had her hands started to shake uncontrollably? Or had she, perhaps…was it possible she had given the wheelchair the merest touch of encouragement?

How about that view? She had asked her mother when they finally reached the top of the Olmsted. How about that?

'Enough,' her mother had said. 'Enough.'

Magazines

– Thea Smiley –

Five days into the summer holidays and Lola had done it all. Any novelty there had been in the timeless hours at home had shrunk and disintegrated like a well-sucked sweet. Finally, the only thing left to do was moan at her mother.

Her mother was in the vegetable patch picking runner beans, the tendrils catching in her hair. She snapped the stalks swiftly and dropped the beans into a colander at her feet. 'Go and see if Sarah's in,' she said.

Lola sighed, blowing her fringe clear of her forehead. 'She's too young.' She took a bean from the colander and crunched through the rough green flesh, her mouth open for full amplification. Her mother edged round to the other side of the canes, and her voice weaved between the leaves.

'She might be in the paddling pool. You could join her. It would cool you down.'

Lola squeezed a bright pink bean from the pod and flicked it into the air. It looked plastic and unnatural against the blue sky, then gleamed like freshly-spat bubble gum among the lettuces. She thought about the paddling pool, and sauntered off towards the garden gate.

The gate was green with algae, and damp beneath her hand. It was fastened by a rusty metal hook. She liked the way it swung open. No other barrier yielded so easily. Every door needed a nudge, and other gates had to be lifted or dragged, but this gate made the world accessible. She opened it, and set off at a gallop down the brick path.

She ran past the disused dairy, the empty hen house, and the garage full of nesting chickens, disobedience shining in their eyes. At the boundary hedge she stopped. The wheat field glowed beneath the high sun and, beside it, the track stretched straight ahead, down to Sarah's house and beyond, to the country lane.

Lola pulled at the grasses along the edge of the track, stripping them of their seeds, leaving the stems waving baldly behind her. The seeds slipped softly through her fingers, caught the warm gusts of summer air, and settled on the verge and in the dust. She watched them fall and wondered what it would be like to float between the ox-eye daisies and drift down into the deep foliage, surrounded by the bitter scent of nettles, down to where the roots gripped the earth.

As she walked, she kicked stones and delighted in the raised dust. A pheasant flapped clumsily from a nearby hedge, and she clapped, simulating the shots which came from the wood at weekends. She rehearsed what she would say to Sarah's mother until the words made no sense at all.

At the bottom of the incline gnats buzzed around a dark, tree-lined ditch. Lola left the track and crossed the gravel drive. She knocked on the door and held her breath as she listened for the usual sounds: the feet on the stairs or Sarah's voice. Nothing. She knocked again and waited. The breeze blew the wind chimes in the apple tree at the end of the garden. She peered towards the lane, but there was no sign of a car.

As she turned to leave, a latch clicked, and Sarah's brother appeared at a first floor window.

'What are you after?' he said, his voice husky.

Lola tucked wild strands of hair behind her ears and asked if Sarah was there. He shook his head.

'Should be home soon.' He leant on the sill and stared at her until her cheeks began to burn. 'Come in and wait, if you want.' She wondered what to do.

Robert was seventeen, possibly eighteen, and had never spoken to her before. Usually he hid in his bedroom, only the rattle of a drum kit indicating his presence. She looked up and was about to reply when he shut the window.

She'd gone as far as the ditch when she heard the front door open. Robert was leaning against the doorframe, something rustling in his hand. He took out a sweet and put it in his mouth, then tilted the packet towards her.

'Have one,' he said, shaking the contents. He looked taller than usual. His closely cropped hair bristled against the paintwork, and he had a speckling of acne on his cheeks. 'Go on,' he urged.

As she walked towards him the scent of his deodorant caught in her throat. She dipped her hand into the packet.

'Thanks,' she said, a dark red wine gum between her fingers. He smiled briefly, baring uneven teeth.

'You can come in, you know,' he said, then went back into the house.

Lola stepped inside. The room smelled strongly of air freshener and there was no sign of Robert. On the carpet near the radiator, a doll peered through a small window cut roughly out of an upturned cardboard box. The make-shift house had no door, and the words 'Stork margarine' were printed on the side like strange graffiti. Nearby another doll lay face-down on a pile of clothes as though exhausted from being endlessly dressed and undressed.

Once, when Lola and Sarah had been playing in the sitting-room, Robert had dangled that doll from an upstairs window, the string tied around its neck. Its plastic arms tapped against the pane as it swung past, naked, its hair on end. Sarah screamed with rage and ran to tell her mother, and Lola caught the sound of distant laughter.

In the kitchen, water thundered into a metal sink. She swallowed. Her mouth was dry, so dry that she felt as though she had eaten a sloe. She was pleased to see Robert enter the room holding a glass of orange squash.

'Sit down, if you want,' he said, as he closed the front door, and she did so. He put the glass on the coffee table between them, then flopped sideways into the armchair, his legs over one arm.

'So,' she said, her voice high and young in the silence. 'Where have they gone?'

'Shops,' he said. He reached for the glass and drained it, his Adam's apple sliding up and down his neck like a yo-yo. Lola tried to look as though she wasn't thirsty, as though she didn't care. She fiddled with a fabric-covered button on the sofa, turning it until the thread strained. Then she looked out at the garden, where the paddling pool slumped in the sun. The blue plastic was streaked with bird droppings, and a washing-up liquid bottle lay in the shallow water. Robert sighed and, for a moment, she thought she could feel his warm breath travel across the room towards her.

'Boring, isn't it?' he said, stretching. Lola nodded and looked at her hands.

Her fingernails were streaked green from the runner bean. Robert shifted in the armchair.

'Do you like magazines?'

'Yes,' she said, and the covers of her favourite magazines flicked through her mind.

'I've got some upstairs if you want to come and see,' he said, and smiled.

Lola followed him up the stairs. The landing was warm and filled with the low buzz of flies, which threw themselves against the skylights. On the wall were family photos: pictures of babies on beaches, Sarah in a nappy and pirate's hat, John, her other brother, on a new bike, and a few of Robert, his face younger, softer. In one photo he was in a canoe. In another he was sitting on a tree stump holding an air rifle, finger on the trigger and his fringe in his eyes. As Lola stared at the photo he called to her from his bedroom.

The room was dimly lit, the curtains closed. There were posters of rock bands on the walls, a dusty drum kit in the corner, and his clothes had been kicked to one side- a tangled high tideline. Scattered around were 'A' level books about chemistry and biology, but there were no magazines. Lola stood near the door while Robert put on some music. Then he sat on the carpet in the lamp-light.

'Sit down then,' he said, pointing to the bed. She perched on the edge, smoothing the covers, and watched as he got up and closed the door, extinguishing the light from the landing. 'These magazines are very special,' he said, as he knelt beside her feet. 'Shut your eyes until I tell you to open them.' She hesitated.

'Shut my eyes?'

'Yes,' he said simply, firmly, and she did so. The bed shook slightly as he leant against it and reached underneath. Something slid across the floor and she heard the flap of turning pages. Slowly, carefully, an open magazine was placed on her lap, the cool, smooth cover curling over her thighs as the spine settled softly in between. She could feel his breath on her knees, and she suspected that, for some reason, he was laughing.

'Can I open my eyes now?' she asked.

'Just a minute,' he said, turning a page. The room seemed hotter, the music louder, and he shifted closer until he was almost sitting on her feet. 'I bet you've never seen anything like this before,' he said. 'Come on, look.'

Lola stared at the shiny pages in her lap and struggled to make sense of the images. The shapes seemed abstract and alien and, briefly, she wondered whether it could be some kind of art. She blinked. Gradually, the shapes rearranged themselves into recognisable forms. Robert began to laugh, loudly this time. Women, pieces of women, their skin, hair, legs, lips, and breasts were spread out in front of her.

'Go on,' he urged, 'have a good look.' He shoved the magazine towards her. She stood up and it fell to the floor. 'You can't go now,' he said, holding her ankle, 'we've only just started.'

'Get off,' she said, jerking her leg away from him. He got up.

'It's all natural. Nothing wrong with it.' Lola pushed at the door. 'Tell you what, we could have some fun,' he said. 'I've got a camera here somewhere.' He began to search his desk and shelves, and paper and pens fell to the floor. But she pulled the door and it opened.

She ran down the stairs. From his room Robert shouted: 'Come on Lola, I want to play.' She crossed the sitting-room, knocking over the cardboard box. The doll toppled out, naked. 'Just one photo,' Robert called, as he jumped down the stairs. Lola grappled with the latch. Glancing behind her, she saw him clambering over the sofa, the camera in his hand. He raised it to his eye. 'Smile,' he said. As he pressed the button she burst out into the sunlight.

Lola didn't stop running until she reached the boundary hedge. Then, with her chest heaving, she glanced back down the track. In the shadows by the tree-lined ditch, Robert stood watching her, his hands in his pockets.

'Go home,' she whispered. But he showed no sign of moving. So she turned and ran past the garage, startling the chickens. She ran past the hen house and the dairy, until she reached the garden gate. She lifted the hook and it swung open, and she hurried through, up the step. Then she closed the gate firmly behind her

Mira/Meera

– Avani Shah –

I heard the Indian accent just as our lavender scones arrived. It was a woman speaking. She didn't talk like my mother, who the kids in my Year Four class used to compare to Apu from *The Simpsons*, but like Aishwarya Rai, almost RP, but softer, sexier. Classier. She sat opposite a grey-haired white woman at the table behind ours, and though I couldn't see her face, the tearoom was so cramped I could have touched her hair and made it look like an accident. It was Indian hair: wiry and puffy at the same time – the type of hair you only got from years of systematically ironing out curls. She was scribbling in a Moleskine, nodding as she wrote, while the white woman spoke. One of her legs was folded underneath her, and her small brown foot poked out through the back of the chair like a tail, bare but for a bronze chappal hooked over the big toe. I wanted to tickle it.

If I were my grandfather, I might have struck up a conversation with the Indian woman. It was something he'd embarrassed me by doing a number of times when I was a kid – whenever he saw another man in a brown suit and trainers, or a woman in a sari. 'Where are you from?' he'd ask them in Gujarati, taking it for granted that they would understand him, before spending a few minutes exchanging pleasantries and finding out who they had in common. This, I'd long decided, wasn't something my generation could do. It meant admitting that your parents once came from somewhere else, that you were different to your friends – a thought that still made me feel prickly. If we'd been home in London, Olivia and I might have invented an elaborate story behind how the young Indian woman and the older white woman came to be drinking tea with one another. But this was Norwich.

'Someone you know, Mira?' Olivia asked me – it was the first time she'd visited.

I shook my head. 'I just haven't heard an Indian accent since I moved here. She must be an -'

'International student?' Olivia guessed.

'And the white lady is probably her tutor.'

Olivia sniffed at my use of the word 'white'. I ignored her.

Some weeks later, I was alone in my room when the website of a local writer called Meera Desai came up on my Twitter feed. In my year at school there had been three other girls called Mira (or Meera), all of them Gujarati, but this was the first time I'd seen someone with my name in Norwich. Her page showed an Indian woman standing beneath a palm tree. She wore tortoiseshell glasses and a pair of denim shorts. Her hair was wiry and puffy at the same time.

Under the photograph was the following bio:

Meera Desai has an MFA from Columbia, and now lives in Norwich, UK, where she is completing a PhD. Her short stories and poetry have appeared in various journals and magazines around the world.

I pictured seeing her again. Instead of the tearoom, which I only frequented when showing Norwich off to visitors, I imagined seeing her at the Oxfam bookshop. Perhaps we'd lock eyes as we both reached for the same Amitav Ghosh book and then step back and laugh. It had to be Amitav Ghosh, I decided, or Arundhati Roy – definitely an author I might later discover she'd also pretended to have read while bluffing a Postcolonialism seminar. We'd engage in a silent back and forth – *'You have it!' 'No, you take it – I insist!'* – but Meera Desai would speak first:

'You like Amitav Ghosh?' She would pronounce his name correctly, the 'v' more like a 'w'. 'But *I* like Amitav Ghosh!'

I'd reply with something impressive – *'Did you know he withdrew from consideration for the Commonwealth Prize?'* – and Meera Desai would suggest meeting up over coffee to talk about books. I'd play it cool. Shrug. 'Sure.' Then I'd write my number in the front of the book, press it back into her hands, and leave the shop without another word.

I wasn't like my grandfather. I went to Brownies instead of Bharatanatyam, German club instead of Gujarati school, and ate Big Macs behind my mother's back. I studied Creative Writing because my mother wanted me to study Law, and after arriving in Norwich I wrote about characters called Jessica, and Lily, and Rose. Now I lost whole afternoons in the tearoom hoping that Meera Desai might come in again. When I visited my parents for Diwali, I stole a pair of my mother's chappals – which I learned were in the Kolhapuri style – and wore them around town despite the October puddles. I bought myself a Moleskine.

My housemates began frustrating me by not being 'Indian' enough. They were proud vegetarians, not grudging ones, who couldn't grasp why I, as an atheist, cited 'Hinduism' as my reason for not eating meat. Meera Desai, I was convinced, would understand. I considered her decision to retweet an already-viral interview with Zadie Smith, my favourite writer, as evidence of our compatibility. After she blogged about spending some time in New Jersey, I hacked into my American cousin's Facebook to see if they had any friends in common (they both knew the three Chauhan brothers – all Rutgers graduates who posted excessively about their cars). When she Instagrammed a cup of tea, I zoomed in on the label at the end of the teabag string and bought myself a box of the same brand. 'You know they're owned by Nestlé,' my housemate Freddie told me.

It was late one afternoon, the tearoom empty, and I was getting ready to leave when Meera Desai walked in. I slid back into my seat. Her hair was shorter, and wet from the rain, but I recognised her tortoiseshell glasses. She was alone. As the waiter approached her I strained to catch her accent, but the coffee machine whistled too loudly. When the waiter left, she glanced at her iPhone, typed something, and then pulled out a pristine copy of *Mrs. Dalloway*. She was different to how I remembered her – it wasn't just her hair. She sat straighter, elbows splayed on the table, feet firmly planted on the ground. When I saw she was wearing Keds, I tucked my chappaled feet out of sight. I spread my books and papers out over the table, the Moleskine in full view, and waited for her to notice me. She didn't look up. The tearoom too felt different. I'd been there when it was empty before, but the lack of chatter that had once felt peaceful, now emphasised sounds I previously hadn't noticed. Somewhere in a back room, a fridge hummed noisily, and overhead floorboards creaked as someone paced in the flat above. On the wall beside me, a cuckoo clock tutted as the seconds passed. I coughed, but still Meera Desai didn't look up.

Ever since I came across Meera Desai's website, I'd daydreamed variations on how we might meet in the Oxfam bookshop. Sometimes we both reached for the same copy of a different book, another time we bumped into each other in the doorway as we both rushed to shelter from the rain, but the one thing all my dreams had in common was that it was always Meera Desai who spoke to me first. After a while, I opened the copy of *White Teeth* I'd been carrying around since she shared the Zadie Smith interview, and every now and then giggled as I turned the pages. From the corner of my eye, I saw her lift her head. I held my breath and waited for her to realise what I was reading – *'Oh Zadie Smith!'* I imagined her calling across the room with a little clap of excitement. *'So witty!'* – but all she did was take a sip of her tea and turn back to *Mrs. Dalloway*. I laughed louder and rustled the pages more than was necessary. Meera Desai put in ear buds.

She placed *Mrs. Dalloway* flat on the table, and hunched over it, letting her hair spill over her face in thick soggy hanks. Under the table, she tapped her foot. I wondered what she was listening to. Every few minutes, she pulled her iPhone towards her to glance at something on the screen, the blue light escaping through her cage of hair; and each time she put the phone back down on the table, she shrunk a little lower in her seat. Her foot jigged faster and faster. One time, she looked at the phone, and then across the room. For a moment, our eyes met. I smiled broadly, but her pupils flicked to the clock on the wall. She turned to the phone again and typed something. I sipped my tea. Her table rumbled. She smiled at the screen and then tucked the phone away in her bag. She lifted her head a little then, and picked *Mrs. Dalloway* back up. That was when I realised she hadn't turned the page once since she'd arrived. The book was new, free from creases, a prop. I stood up. My chappals slapped on the wooden floor, but her earbuds meant she didn't hear me approaching. She jumped when I tapped her on the shoulder. *Can I help you?* she signalled with her eyebrows as she pulled out an earbud.

It wasn't until she winced that I realised I'd spoken to her in Gujarati. Something about the way her lip curled made me think she understood, but she remained silent.

I tried again. 'I was just – uh – I was just wondering where in India you were from?'

She said nothing for a few moments. Then she shifted her chair an inch or two away. 'I'm sorry,' she said. 'Do I know you?' Her accent was cool, confident. American.

'I've seen you on Twitter,' I blurted. 'My name's Mira too.'

'Oh. Right.'

Behind us the door creaked open.

Meera Desai unfurled. She sat straighter. She smoothed her hair out, and then her T-shirt. She slotted one ankle daintily behind the other. On the table she arranged her cup and saucer and then placed *Mrs. Dalloway* page down in a tent shape so that it was open about half-way through. She smiled with her teeth. I smiled too. She fingered a loose curl of hair. She waved. I waved back.

'So sorry I'm late!' A blonde woman was standing beside me. 'You won't *believe* what happened!'

Meera Desai laughed and gestured for the blonde woman to sit. The woman dumped a large brown handbag on the table, accidently rumpling the corner of *Mrs. Dalloway*, and then hung her red coat on the back of a chair. As she pulled the chair out to sit down, she turned to me. 'Earl Grey please. Milk on the side.'

I don't remember if I said anything before I ran out of the tearoom, or when exactly I knew that the Meera Desai I'd spent so much time thinking about wasn't the woman I'd overheard the weekend Olivia visited. I stood in the rain for a moment or two, my bare toes splattered with puddle mud, and watched Meera Desai laugh animatedly at the story her blonde friend was telling. Steam rose in circles from their teacups, and orange fairy lights twinkled in the tearoom window. On the way home I stopped at the corner shop and bought a box of teabags from a brand Freddie would approve of. The server reminded me of my mother. 'Thank you,' she said as I left the shop, 'come again.'

Trouble And Strife

– Jenny Ayres –

Dramatis Personae

BREN – a station mistress, in her late thirties

CHORUS – four female performers, of varying ages,
who remain on stage throughout

<u>Setting</u>

A train station.

<u>Year</u>

1942.

Lights up slowly.

CHORUS: A Hertfordshire village sleeps under a sparkling camouflage of white. A blanket of peace unrolling along the rooftops and settling fat and thick on the doorsteps, lacing the inside of every window pane with an antimacassar of ice, as the evacuees pull their eiderdowns tight, knowing the call for a meagre, marmalade-less breakfast is still hours away.

It is a snoozing stillness only the magpies see, as they cut a shape across the sky that, for once, nobody fears. Up over the railway bridge, up over the silver arteries that run in tandem from London to Peterborough, up over the winding paths of Knebworth where the noise of the day has not yet started.

For all, that is, except a small dark figure leaving footprints in the snow,

Walking carefully,

Oh, so carefully,

Stepping, edging her way,

Walking on thin ice, some would say,

Down the road ...

Towards the train station.

The sound of repeated banging, before the ticket office door bursts open. Enter BREN.

BREN: Oh damn it! Bloody door! It's been sticking since before Christmas, but this morning it took several hard shoves, a couple of kicks and a little help from the milk churn on the step before it would shift. *(Brushing herself down and then noticing her coat.)* Oh, but will you look at that? The door handle's caught on my sleeve and ripped a hole right through. Damn thing!

(Unlocking the platform door and opening up the ticket office window.) Do you remember what you said to me, Fred? 'You can handle this place for me, Bren, just 'til I get back, mind, it's not as if it's Kings Cross now, is it?' Well, would you have it any other way? As soon as you knew us women were being conscripted to work, that was that. 'I'm sure you can just about keep the place standing,' you said. Cheeky sod.

(Getting out the station log.) I'm still doing everything just as you showed me - stacking the parcels, right to left, winding the clock, not too tight, and keeping the station log. Now, where are we … oh, yes, the 19th January. Four weeks to the day… Even your flat cap in the hallway doesn't smell of Brylcreem anymore.

I tell you, John and Agnes have been so kind. Always looking out for me. As if they aren't busy enough as it is. What with them taking in an evacuee this last week, and Alec too, they still find time to bring me vegetables from their allotment. John tells me that little Alec has decided he wants to be a train driver when he grows up, but John hasn't the heart to tell him, what with him needing glasses already, he won't be able to drive. He'll just have to make do with firing like his dad. Well, it's still a life on the footplate, isn't it?

CHORUS: A gush of cold wind suddenly knocks the platform door wide open, bringing with it the clackety-clack of the approaching express. Proudly coughing its white plumage up into the sky, with a pop, pop, pop that trails a mass of whisping, white locks. The 6:15 bites its way up the track spitting its dirt and ripping its thundering, rib-rattling wagons through the platform in a blur, before it evaporates back into the morning mist. The first non-stopper.

Sound of a train fading into the distance.

BREN: *(On the platform, shovelling the snow.)* The village looks a real picture today, Fred. Your favourite view from the up platform, here, is a beauty. The school, the high street with the coaches parked up all tidy, and the church, too – all iced like a cake. Well, pretty as it is, I thought I'd better clear these platforms off or someone is sure to come a cropper! Most likely me. *(Putting down the shovel and checking her watch.)* Here it comes, bang on time. *(She picks up the wheelbarrow by her side.)*

CHORUS: 6:21. The paper train. Bringing news, bravery and morale. Hissing to a stop. Doors flung open. Bundles out. Barrow back and forth and then it's gone with a whistle, a slam, a tip of the hat and a wave of the flag. And whilst the newspaper bundles get piled high in the barn, the 6:43 express, rushes through.

BREN: *(Tipping up the barrow.)* Right. Time to wake up the waiting room damp. Now, where did I put those keys? *(Returning to the booking office.)* I need to polish the brass today too. You wouldn't believe this, Fred, but Mrs Garner, the waiting room attendant at Hitchin Station, says the blacked-out windows are as good an

excuse as any not to have to worry about the dust and dirt, but
I don't agree and I know you wouldn't, either. You were always
so proud of your station and, well, wouldn't the Germans just
be celebrating in the streets if they thought we were lowering
our standards?*(Looking around the office.)* Now, where are those
keys? I should really find a place for them, shouldn't I? Oh,
hang on a minute! *(Looking under the counter.)* If I remember
rightly … aha, here they are!

Sound of a train arriving.

CHORUS: 7:24. The first passenger train of the day chunders into
the station and stops. Just a few season-ticket holders on
the way to the Big Smoke and, as the train doors swing
wide on their hinges, they free a mass of dirty footprints
across the remaining crisp snow.

BREN: *(On the platform, checking tickets.)* Mind your step, now, please. It's
still slippy.

A single CHORUS member staggers away from the others, wearing a soldier's uniform.

CHORUS: *(Addressing BREN with slurred speech.)* Excuse me, miss, you got a
cigarette?

BREN: No sorry, sir, I don't. Are you ok?

CHORUS: Where am I?

BREN: This is Knebworth Station.

CHORUS: I think I need to go home …

BREN: And where is that exactly?

CHORUS: Welwyn Garden City. I'm only back a week.

BREN: That is still two stops away, sir. You need to get back on this train. Here, give me your arm.

CHORUS: I'll give you a kiss.

BREN: The train needs to leave.

CHORUS: You're so pretty. Such a pretty … face. What are you doing here?

BREN: I'm working.

CHORUS: Oh, so you're one of those, are you? *(Winks, then whispers.)* How much do you charge?

BREN: I'm the station mistress.

CHORUS: Eh? You don't look like … a stationmustruss … a stustionmustruss … a stussion …

A second CHORUS member comes to stand next to BREN.

CHORUS: You alright there, Brenda?

BREN: John!

CHORUS: You look like you've got your hands full, our girl?

BREN: Oh, he doesn't mean any harm. Help me get him back into the

254

carriage, will you?

CHORUS: *(Taking the soldier's arm.)* Come on, mate. Now, where is it you want to go? *(Both CHORUS members turn away.)*

BREN blows her whistle. Sound of a train departing.

CHORUS: And, before long, the morning sunlight dims into the afternoon hush, once the post has been opened, windows wiped with vinegar and the waiting rooms swept, too. Then there's just enough time to catch up on the station log.

BREN: *(Sat in the booking office, writing.)* That soldier this morning was only blowing off a bit of steam, like so many of our boys back on leave. I'm sure you of all people would understand that, Fred? But there was no way I was going to get him on that train on my own. Thank goodness John was watching from the cab and jumped down to help me.

Everyone tells me what a mighty fine station master you were. As if I didn't know that already. No-one messed with you. But then you always did what you believed was right and just because you were in a reserved profession, well, that was no reason enough for you not to go and do your bit at the front, was it? Being a healthy, strong man as you are. You always cut such a handsome figure on this platform. I hope Monty is looking after you, wherever you are.

(Rubbing her hands together for warmth.) I tell you what, I wouldn't mind your big coat now. I hoped they'd send me another when you handed yours back but all they sent out was an LNER badge. And my own coat will need patching. And, well, what

with this morning and all, it got me thinking, Fred, shouldn't I have a company coat like you?

BREN pauses then, taking a note from the noticeboard, she picks up the telephone receiver and dials.

BREN: Good afternoon. Is that Mr Potten? This is Station Mistress Appleton from Knebworth Station. Can you hear me? "Hello," I said. Yes, I'd like to put in a request.

***

The sound of a train rushing through the station.

CHORUS: And the days travel on into the freezing February rain.

6:15. The non-stopper.

6:21. The paper train.

6:43. The express.

BREN: *(On the platform.)* Stand back, please! Everyone stand back!

A CHORUS member steps apart from the others, and waves to BREN, before addressing her directly.

BREN: Afternoon, Agnes! I saw your John up and out on the 7:24 this morning. He can't have had his twelve hours rest. Could he?

CHORUS: Oh, he's used to it, Bren.

BREN: You off somewhere nice?

CHORUS: Just to the Welwyn Stores on the forty-five minutes past. It's our Alec's sixth birthday on the twentieth of next month and I've saved up some coupons. I'm on the lookout for something special.

BREN: You must be forever rushed off your feet with Thomas, now, as well?

CHORUS: Oh, he's no trouble. Seems everyone along Pondcroft Road has taken in at least one evacuee by now and Alec is always finding new games to show him. He's sleeping better, too, since he started sharing his room. Makes him less afraid of the dark. How are things here?

BREN: Cold.

CHORUS: Oh, Bren. Any news on your coat?

BREN: I've written to the LNER offices but I've not had much luck. Seems they only issue new coats to male employees.

CHORUS: Well, you should tell them your bones are bitten by the cold just the same as any man's.

BREN: That's why I wrote again to a Mr Smithson, this time, at Head Office to say that a secondhand coat would suffice. Turns out they won't give me that, either.

CHORUS: John says you should ring the local union representative. Although you're more than welcome to borrow my other coat in the meantime, you know?

BREN: Thank you but I don't want to be of any trouble. Not to you,

Agnes.

CHORUS:　　Never! I'll get John to bring it down later. If you ever need us, you know where we are, Bren. Anytime, you understand?

BREN:　　Yes. Thank you. *(Noticing.)* That'll be your train.

Sound of a train approaching. BREN blows the whistle.

***

CHORUS:　　Tick tock, tick tock - aching delays are stretching the days now.

3:44

3:45

3:46 and 7 and 8 and...

Finally, here comes the mail train making it through. Barrows to load. Sacks tied tight. Paper and ink offer comfort at night.

BREN:　　*(On the platform, lifting the mailbags.)* I'm sure there's more letters than there used to be - and it's not just because it's Valentine's Saturday, either. Not that war stops the heart. I've known the bomb girls leave notes for their soldiers down the sides of the seats before now. Seems everyone's hoping for a message.

(In the office, unloading the sacks.) It's been exactly three weeks and three days since your last letter, Fred, and nearly two whole months since you left. We've never been apart this long. Do

you remember when we first started courting? You brought me some violets from over the field and asked father, all nicely, if we could go out on a picnic … he wasn't sure but you talked him round. You were always good at that. It felt like that summer would never end. Lying in the warm grass, we watched the birds. Some of them were even bold enough to land on the ground beside us. You knew all the right names for them and I pretended I did too. Then I just closed my eyes and listened to the sound of your chest under my head and the smell of your cotton shirt … Send something soon, Fred. I miss you.

CHORUS: 4:29. Running to time.

4:56. Re-routed.

5:35. Arrives. Twenty-nine minutes late.

One CHORUS member appears at the ticket office window and addresses BREN directly.

CHORUS: Excuse me?

BREN: *(Turning to look.)* Yes.

CHORUS: Station Mistress Appleton?

BREN: Yes.

CHORUS: I'm Officer Leatherson from the Department of Welfare with the LNER – do you   have a few moments, please?

BREN: Of course. *(Opening the office door.)* Please, come round.

CHORUS: What a delightful little station this is. How are you finding things, Mrs. Appleton?

BREN: Just fine, thank you, Mrs Leatherson.

CHORUS: <u>Miss</u> Leatherson.

BREN: Oh, right. Can I get you a cup of tea?

CHORUS: Well, that would be lovely, thank you.

BREN gestures for her to take a seat.

CHORUS: *(Sitting.)* Mrs Appleton, don't be alarmed by my visit, it is simply a routine check. The responsibility has been bestowed to me, as Welfare Officer, to ensure that all our women recruits are content in their new roles. It can be a shock to the system for some. *(Looking around her.)* The lifting - none of it too heavy for you?

BREN: No. I'm fitter than ever.

CHORUS: And you are obviously keeping everything spic and span in here, which is excellent to see.

BREN: I do my best.

CHORUS: Well, we can't ask for any more than that, can we? *(She makes a note and then looks up.)* Now, coming on to the matter of your uniform request ...

BREN: Yes?

CHORUS: We all understand your predicament, of course, but you must have been told quite clearly that company coats are only issued/

BREN: *(Completing her sentence.)* To men. Yes, I know but/

CHORUS: *(Continuing.)* The railways are currently under a huge amount of pressure, Mrs Appleton, of which I'm sure you are aware. I'm afraid the expectation that rules can be rewritten, at this incredibly testing time, when they have worked perfectly well for many years is, shall we say… a little unrealistic? Please stop me, by the way, if you're not following.

BREN: It's just/

CHORUS: *(Interrupting.)* And to be honest, Mrs. Appleton, we are all incredibly conscious that women working <u>on</u> our railways is simply a temporary measure. Do you see?

BREN: *(Pause.)* I see.

CHORUS: *(Returning to her notes.)* Now, was there anything else?

***

The sound of a train passing.

CHORUS: And the March mornings bring a razor sharp cold wind, that carry the shrill laughter of school children running down the station hill, past Mrs Morris, the postwoman, doing her rounds on her bicycle,   and on through the ticket office, where each train brings more passengers, more news.

8.51. Have you heard they're sending more evacuees our way?

No, when'll that be, then?

Anytime now. There was a terrible night raid over Ally Pally last night.

BREN: *(Lifting the telephone receiver and speaking.)* Good morning, switchboard. Yes, can I have the National Union Railways, Hertfordshire Branch, please?

The sound of a train passing. BREN sits waiting on the telephone line.

CHORUS: 10. 32. They're loading up our trains with weapons, so they say, not even the drivers know what's on board.

That'll be what's causing all these delays.

Yes, that and all the troop trains they're running now.

BREN: *(Into the telephone.)* Yes, this is Station Mistress Appleton. Yes. No, not Apsley, Appleton – A – P – P – L - E …yes, that's right.

The sound of another train passing, BREN continues to wait, phone to her ear.

CHORUS: 11.29. What was the last train to come through here?

Is the 11.59 running at all?

Who knows? We've just been told to listen out and wait.

The CHORUS stand and wait on the platform.

BREN: *(Into the telephone.)* Yes, that's right. I rang before about a uniform matter, do you recall?

CHORUS: Wait for announcements.

BREN: Yes, well, I'd like to talk to the person in charge.

CHORUS: Wait for announcements.

BREN: I've already put an official complaint in writing.

CHORUS: Wait for announcements.

BREN: But I haven't got a response.

CHORUS: No further announcements.

BREN: I understand.

The CHORUS sigh and walk away. BREN puts down the receiver.

The sound of a train disappearing into the distance.

***

CHORUS: Whilst the evening light lingers for a little longer now, the last few office workers still shuffle towards home, grey and sleepy. Many rocked to a slumber by the dusty bench seats of the 6:51, snoozing whilst the dark draws over the crisscrossing tracks, the backyards with washing still on the line, the bike left by the gate.

BREN: *(On the platform, wearing another non-uniform coat, loading parcels onto* *the barrow.)* Bloody evening. Bloody parcel train. Three hours late again. It's worse this month than last. Can't be helped, but it's hard to see the addresses in the dark.

I try not to worry myself that you haven't written for seven weeks, Fred, but it seems like an awfully long time … I don't know what to think? My letters haven't been returned, so that's something. Lucy Miller, the goods porter at Finsbury Park, got a whole bundle of letters for her sweetheart sent back. Unopened. That can only be bad news, can't it?

I tell you, it's Alec's birthday later this month. You'd know what to get him, wouldn't you? I thought maybe a toy train? I want to get something nice, especially now I've got Agnes' coat. Although I fear for my life I'll ruin it, not being designed for work as it is.

Oh, my hands are like leather and my fingertips are cracking but I can't do the tickets with my gloves on … Ouch! Another bloody paper cut – why don't people fold down their edges? Oh, I better find something to wrap this in.

One CHORUS member moves nearer to BREN and clears her throat.

CHORUS: You not got a home to go to, Brenda?

BREN: Mrs Morris, I didn't see you there. Can't finish until I get these parcels done, can I? Oh, have you got something for me?

CHORUS: *(Handing over a pile of letters.)* You're my last delivery of the day.

BREN looks through the letters and then tears one open quickly.

CHORUS: Any good news?

BREN: No, it's just … it's a work matter. I can tell by the letterhead. It's not what I was hoping for.

CHORUS: Not to worry, I'm sure you'll hear something soon. I've heard the mail services abroad are nowhere near as good as our own postal system.

BREN: Have you heard anything from Stan?

CHORUS: Not enough, but he seems to be okay. As far as I can tell. He wouldn't want to worry his old mum. He lost his best friend a couple of weeks back, but he doesn't talk about it in his letters. I always thought he was too soft for war. I'm knitting him some socks. Makes me feel I'm doing something. Oh, your hand's bleeding!

BREN: It's fine, I'll put my hanky around it. I need to get these parcels finished.

CHORUS: Would you like me to take your letters into the office?

BREN: *(Handing the letters back.)* Might as well. Thank you.

CHORUS: *(Looking down at the opened letter on top of the pile.)* As you know, I'm not one to pry, but …

BREN: Oh, I have no secrets, Mrs Morris. It'll be another refusal letter about my uniform. It always is. Read it aloud to me if you like. I don't mind. That way I can carry on with this. *(BREN continues working.)*

CHORUS: Of course! *(Keenly taking the letter to the lamp, she puts on her reading glasses and clears her throat again.)* Now, let me see. "Dear Station Mistress Appleton. After our lengthy telephone communications, I can inform you that your request has been referred to the chief of the National Union Rail Authority, who will endeavour to look into this matter forthwith."

BREN: Just the same as the last letter.

CHORUS: *(Continuing.)* "A meeting has been arranged on Friday 20th March, at 9am, at our Central London offices to summarise our findings. Present will be Mr. S. Pitson, Manager of the NUR, Hertfordshire and Miss M. Leatherson, Senior Welfare Officer of the LNER."

BREN stops and looks up.

"Your complaint has been considered and discussed with much seriousness and we intend this meeting to be the conclusion of this matter. I would, therefore, be very grateful if you could confirm your attendance at your earliest convenience."

BREN: Well, I never! Called into the London offices, eh? What would Fred think? Not that I could ever leave the station on a weekday morning, there's no relief staff and we're all working double shifts as it is. And they'd know that. Mind, Agnes will be pleased I'm making a little progress, I suppose. Oh well, Mrs Morris, what can I say? *(BREN sighs, takes back the letters, puts them on top of the parcels in the barrow and wheels it into the office.)*

***

Sound of a train rushing past.

CHORUS: And the days pass through the week. Wind up the clock. Wind up the clock. Rushing windows carry blank faces up and down the line, whilst special trains, hiding behind the sagging timetable, tug at your hair and pull at your clothes to follow them to a destination undisclosed, at top secret speeds where the trees all blur into one.

4:56. Waiting to depart.

5:35. Delayed. Then cancelled.

6:39. Severely delayed.

CHORUS: *(On the platform, as a passenger.)* Is the train to London going to arrive at all?

BREN: I have no reason to believe that the 6:39 isn't running, sir, but there are still two expresses to come through yet.

CHORUS: Suddenly the sirens start. Quietly at first, then louder as the alerts run up the line. Night has fallen and brought its deadly shapes over the tracks. Watch out in the Blackout!

BREN: Clear the platform, please! Clear the platform! Everyone inside now. Hurry.

CHORUS: Keep them moving. Stick to your post.

BREN: This way, please. Quickly! Quickly! Is there anyone else? Get inside the waiting room, as quickly as you can.

CHORUS: Where is my luggage?

BREN: Don't worry about that now, madam. Please just get inside.

CHORUS: I want my bag.

BREN: You need to get inside. For your own safety. *(Calling into the waiting room.)* Everyone please stay here. There isn't enough time to get to the shelter now. You must wait inside until the alert is over.

CHORUS: Wait for the boom and the rattle that rumbles your guts and makes the spit dry in your mouth. A room full of people, standing in darkness, with their tickets in their breast pockets being punched by their pounding hearts.

And slowly, down the line, the approaching express creeps forward down the permanent way – permanent in nothing but name and hope. In the thick darkness the driver tries to feel the curves in the tracks, like the veins in his arms, whilst the fireman shovels coal into the firebox, feeding the angry glow.

BREN: *(Looking out over the village to the horizon.)* It's not a false alarm this time, Fred. There are explosions only a little way off, now. The sky's turned orange and I can see tunnels of black smoke rising up somewhere over Welwyn.

CHORUS: The cab shakes on the tracks. The gate rattles.

BREN: Are they getting closer? Please, God, no.

CHORUS: A blue flash and a rage of sound, buzzes and explodes, pulsing through Brenda's neck and raging down her back and legs, knocking her flat to the ground.

BREN: *(Coughing and spitting gravel from her mouth.)* Jesus Christ! *(Scrambling to her feet.)* Oh, Fred, it looks as if something's on fire in the village. It's hard to see over the trees. Jesus! Is that screaming? Please let everyone be alright. Please. My ears are ringing. Here's the express coming through, but no, wait, it's starting to brake. Something's wrong … it's slowing. Keep them moving. Keep them moving. We all know that. It's not meant to stop here. What are they doing? What's wrong?

CHORUS: The train rattles its soot into the station and stops. Then, somewhere in the cloud of dirt and darkness, there are running footsteps along the platform edge.

BREN: Hello? *(Calling down the platform.)* Who's that? Driver, is that you? What's happened?

CHORUS: *(A CHORUS member rushes towards BREN.)* Is this your station? We need to stop.

BREN: Yes. Why?

CHORUS: My fireman's badly shaken. It was a close hit.

BREN: What? They've hit the tracks?

CHORUS: No, close by.

BREN: Where? I can't see from here.

CHORUS: Pondcroft Road, so I'm told.

BREN: Oh, no. Are you sure?

CHORUS: We got a clear view from the train.

BREN: Shall I call/

CHORUS: *(Interrupting.)* The telephone lines will be down.

BREN: Where is he?

CHORUS: He shouldn't have been working at all, he wasn't scheduled for this train, but there was no-one else. He's standing by the cab. He said he needed to stop.

BREN: Why?

CHORUS: He said he's local.

BREN: Oh, no! *(Running down the platform, calling.)* John! John! Is that you?

BREN *runs towards another CHORUS member, John, standing alone, his eyes down. She slows as she recognises him.*

BREN: Oh John! Are you ok?

No response.

BREN: John?

CHORUS: John strikes a match, a tiny furnace in the darkness, and takes it towards a cigarette hanging limply from his lips. Slowly. Silently. The match, now inside a curled hand, brings a small spotlight up into a hollow, dirty face. He inhales. A soot-smeared statue. He doesn't speak. He doesn't look up.

Nothing to say. Nothing to be seen. Nothing, that is, except two thin silver lines that have traced themselves silently through the dirt of each cheek to his chin. He swallows. He makes no sound. He shakes the match out. The face is gone.

Brenda found out later that night, that the whole south end of Pondcroft Road was bombed out. John finished his shift and came home. To nothing. Agnes, Alec and Thomas. All gone. But he knew that already. He knew the moment he saw. Of course, he did. He was a fireman. He'd worked with fire all his life.

***

Sound of a train fading into the distance.

CHORUS: The fragile grey ash of the morning finally arrives, bruised and quiet. The 'All Clear' came in the early hours when they sent the maintenance and track repair workers out but, as if by some small miracle, the tracks were virtually untouched.

Nothing to stop the trains that begin another day. Everyone with a job to do, a duty to fill. And as the sun edges up, there is a small dark figure making her way down the hill.

Slowly.

271

Tentatively.

With a face like snow.

Key in the lock, another shove and push. And –

BREN enters the office.

BREN: Someone needs to have a look at this door.

CHORUS: She says that every morning now.

The gasping cold March wind blows through the booking office, but only the dust on the floor feels like dancing. The grey sunlight pushes through the window and across the clock face. Ticking. Across the papers and mail basket. Empty. Across the counter, bare and smooth. Waiting. Through the yellowing glass of the oil lamp onto the desk, casting a shadow on a present wrapped and ready with a bow - a toy train.

BREN lifts the telephone receiver and listens.

BREN: Nothing. *(She replaces the receiver and takes out the station log. She starts to write.)* 20th of March. *(She stops, staring at the blank page and then closes it again.)* I caught sight of myself in the mirror above the mantle, and I thought - you look old, Bren. And I do. I don't think you'd recognise me, Fred. Oh, what I would give to see you. For you to hold me. At least, to read a few of your words - that I may know you are still in this world and that I will rest my head on your chest again, hear your heart beat, that more remains of us than just the sound of me saying your name.

BREN *slowly walks out onto the platform.*

> You can see so much of our village from here. The damage done last night.

Sound of a train quietly in the distance.

CHORUS: 6:43. Here comes the express. The ever-clanking, continuity of a network that never grieves.

BREN: Does it never end?

The train grows louder. BREN *moves towards the platform edge.*

BREN: Milk churns arriving and crates of beer for the pub,
Parcels, papers and packages too.

CHORUS: The whooshing, shaking beast shrieks its whistle down the track.

BREN: Livestock, as well, and evacuees waiting,
All need to be unloaded, counted and put on the cart.

The train builds to a crescendo.

CHORUS: Two small feet on the platform edge,

BREN: Tickets checked, lost property found,
Counting the cashbox and lighting the lamps.

CHORUS: Balancing on a long white line.

BREN: And passengers asking, forgetting, rushing and lost,
Are always greeted with a smile in the cold, forever dirt of it all.

CHORUS: She closes her eyes. Lets the train rattle her bones.

The train starts to fade slowly into the distance.

BREN: *(Slowly opening her eyes.)* And through it all a station mistress wears her company badge, and when the snow, rain and even bombs start to fall she stands tall on her platform. Why? Why, when her world is falling apart in front of her very eyes? Why, when everything she knows is gone? When everything that matters is shattered. Because for every moment she risks her life, she is playing her own part in this war. In these terrible, terrible times of strife.

She steps back from the platform edge.

I don't know what you would think of me, Fred, but I wanted to be in London today to go to that meeting. Part of me hoped you would be proud of me. But they refused my leave. Perhaps they're right. After all, on this day of all days, there is nothing that needs to be done more than station work. Knebworth needs its station. And there is nothing more left to me now than just enough time to get everything opened up,

CHORUS: on this day of all days.

BREN: To get back to the ticket office,

CHORUS: on this day of all days.

BREN: To sweep the waiting rooms,

CHORUS: on this day of all days.

BREN: And to think of nothing but my place here. *(Looking down at the coat she is wearing.)* I couldn't bear to damage this now. *(She takes it off and holds it to her.)* Oh, Agnes.

BREN returns to the office and gently hangs up Agnes' coat, putting on her own torn coat instead.

CHORUS: Time to start the day. To find the ladder and cut the vine that hangs over the ticket office, like tangled eyebrows over tired eyes. To fetch the barrow for the papers that are already on the platform waiting. To do what she feels she must.

But then, there's the sound of a bicycle bell.

One CHORUS member steps forward from the others, calling.

CHORUS: Brenda, Brenda!

BREN: Mrs Morris?

CHORUS: I've got a letter for you, Brenda.

BREN: Addressed to me or the station?

CHORUS: To you.

BREN: Handwritten?

CHORUS: Yes.

BREN: But the mail train hasn't arrived yet -

CHORUS: It's not today's mail. It's yesterday's - we couldn't get it out before the raid came. Anyway, I thought there's no point it just sitting in the office looking at me, when I could easily cycle it up. *(She hands BREN the letter.)* Knowing that you were waiting for news.

BREN *takes a deep breath, then rips the envelope open quickly, with shaking hands.*

BREN: It's not his handwriting.

CHORUS: What is it?

BREN: *(Reading aloud.)*

"Dear Station Mistress Appleton

We wanted you to have the enclosed. The details of your situation have been up and down the line and we thought this might help. You are a station mistress, after all, and, knowing that a station never closes without good cause, Porter Lewison from Huntingdon and Booking Office Clerk Jones from Arlesey have agreed to be along on the 7:24 to staff Knebworth Station on 20th of this month. This way you may attend this vital, unprecedented meeting, of which we have all been told about, and for which you have fought so hard on behalf of us all. We are incredibly grateful for your efforts, for you have found the courage within us we never knew we had.

And, whilst the work of British Railways must continue, if

there is one thing the LNER railway women pride themselves on, it's working together. On this day of all days.

Yours sincerely

CHORUS:

One CHORUS member steps forward, revealing her company badge.

Mrs. Garner, Waiting Room Attendant, Hitchin Station.

Another CHORUS member steps forward, revealing her company badge.

Lucy Miller, Goods Porter, Finsbury Park.

Another CHORUS member steps forward, revealing her company badge.

Margaret M. Smithson, Booking Clerk, Letchworth Garden City.

The last CHORUS member steps forward, revealing her company badge.

Edna Watkinson, Signal Woman, Alexandra Palace.

Bren turns over the pages of the letter.

BREN: It's a petition. 74 names. 74 railway women. A petition for my company coat.

CHORUS: A small dark figure stands on the up platform of Knebworth Station and waits for the next train to London. She shivers, looking north up the track for the first sign of the big round smoke box, snorting its approach. The 7:24.

She stands alone on the same platform where she leant up and kissed her husband goodbye through an open train window as it slowly carried him away. She waits, as the magpies circle overhead before flying on over the station lane where a postwoman is making her way back to the office, past a barking dog and the baker's window, where preparations have begun for a village that will, today, be hungrier and busier than ever.

She waits. A lone figure on an empty platform. Another traveller with a journey to make, but in her hand she holds a letter.

Slow fade to black.

Sound of a train approaching in the distance.

End.

End Note:

Whilst all the names in this story are fictional, the events are based on the true account of Crossing Keeper Davison(i), from Hartlepool, who spent two years, from 1945, campaigning for the LNER to issue her with a company coat. She never received one. Today over six thousand women work as travel assistants on British Railways(ii). They all wear their company's issued uniform.

Acknowledgments

First, and foremost, enormous thanks must go to my husband, Trev, for his continuing encouragement, patience and forever astute script-editing skills. Thanks also to my mum, Barb, and sister, Melly, for all their feedback and ideas, as well as my sister-in-law, Val, for her dedicated researching and to my two children, Joe and Ella, for allowing 'Mummy' to be, and do, something else for a little while.

Thanks go to Ann Judge for sharing her detailed historical research of Knebworth, along with Anne and Ian Purvis, Tone Nobay, Jo Simson and Clare Fleck for their local knowledge and resource ideas, and to Bill, Grace and Martin Smith for offering invaluable insight into the life of a fireman in Hertfordshire, during World War Two. Thanks, also, to Richard Camp for sharing his knowledge of the London to Peterborough railway line, and to my dad, Brian, Dave Carter and David Betchetti for sharing their memories of Knebworth Station and a childhood around the railway.

Thanks, of course, to Words and Women for giving me this fantastic opportunity and for the guidance to take this script in a new direction.

Last, but by no means least, thanks to both my nans, who both played their own part in the last World War and whose lives, and constant love, have always been an inspiration to me – this play is dedicated to you both.

(i)Wojtczak, H. (2005) Railwaywomen, (The Hastings Press), p187

(ii)Office for National Statistics. (2014) Annual Survey of Hours and Earnings - Provisional Results.

Contributors

Tricia Abraham is originally from the Caribbean but has lived in Cambridge for the past eleven years. She has an MA in Creative Writing and initially wrote for stage and film. She started to experiment with the short story format when she moved to the U.K. and wanted to reminisce about her cultural memories.

Melinda Appleby won Country Living's Best Writer Award in 2011 and gained an MA (Distinction) in Wild Writing (Essex University) in 2014. Her poems have been published in a fenland anthology and *Earthlines*, and she has an essay in *Est*, the new book of East Anglian writing. Melinda runs a creative writing programme, 'Sandlines', with fellow Words & Women writer and artist, Lois Williams.

Jenny Ayres is a north Hertfordshire based writer, actress and mum. After studying at The Central School of Speech and Drama, Jenny was invited onto the Royal Court Young Writers Programme and in 2005 won the London Lost Theatre Festival with her one woman show 'The Fourth Photo'. Jenny then travelled to Milan and Budapest, where she was commissioned to write two short films, before her first story, '...but that's who you are', was published in 2007. Jenny recently worked as Writing Director for a theatre project entitled 'Through a Child's Eyes', in conjunction with Letchworth Arts Centre.

Sarah Baxter returned to Colchester, the town of her birth, a decade ago after living in Australia and Scotland. Sarah's flash fictions have been published in the Bridport Prize anthology, and online by *InkTears* and *Flash500*. In 2014, Sarah's work-in-progress first novel was longlisted for the Crime Writers' Association's Debut Dagger prize and went on to win A.M Heath's Criminal Lines competition.

Lynne Bryan is the author of a short story collection, "Envy At The Cheese Handout" (published by Faber & Faber), and the novels 'Gorgeous' and 'Like Rabbits' (Sceptre). Her work has been included in many anthologies and has been broadcast on the radio and adapted for film. She is co-organiser of Words And Women.

Ceridwen Edwards (aka. Satyagita) was born in Great Yarmouth in 1958. She's a practising Buddhist and writes to try and make sense of the world. She wrote her first book when she was five, 'Wendy And The Witch'.

Louise Ells has a Creative Writing MA from Bath Spa University and is now pursuing a PhD at Anglia Ruskin University. Her thesis comprises 'Lacunae', a collection of thematically linked short stories, and a critical commentary examining Alice Munro's revision strategies in 'Dear Life'. She's recently had stories published in *The Masters Review* and *Harts & Minds*.

Abby Erwin spent the first eighteen years of her life in India, Germany and the Czech Republic. She now lives in Norwich in a state of perpetual culture shock and is studying for an MA in Creative Writing at the University of East Anglia.

Lilie Ferrari was co-creator and writer for the medical drama series 'The Clinic' for RTE, and has written episodes of 'Peak Practice' (Carlton), 'Dangerfield' (BBC), 'Casualty' (BBC), 'Berkeley Square' (BBC), 'Holby '(BBC) and numerous episodes of 'EastEnders' (BBC). She co-created storylines for the returning series of 'Crossroads', winning the ITV commission for Carlton Productions. She's also storylined for 'Family Affairs' (Channel 5), and 'Playing the Field' for Tiger Aspect/BBC. Lilie's also had four novels published, and is currently working on her fifth.

Melissa Fu is writing a collection of memoir-style pieces based on growing up in the Rocky Mountains. She's an active member of the Angles writing workshop, based in Cambridge. In 2014, she started leading and facilitating Writing Circles, small writing groups in Cambridgeshire designed to create community and cultivate writers' voices.

Hannah Garrard is currently studying for an MA in Biography and Creative Non-Fiction at the UEA, where she also took her undergraduate degree in English Literature in 2005. She's worked as a teacher in East Asia and West Africa, but Norwich is a place she always seems to come back to. Her writing has appeared in the *Guardian*, *New Internationalist* and *Going Down Swinging*.

Belona Greenwood is a former journalist who escaped to Norwich where she did an MA in Scriptwriting at the University of East Anglia. She has won an Escalator award for creative non-fiction, is a winner of the Decibel Penguin prize for life-writing and writes plays for adults and children. She is a Director of Chalk Circle Theatre Company, and founder and co-organiser of Words And Women.

Hannah Harper was born in Reading and studied literature at the University of Sheffield and creative writing at the UEA. She's worked as a receptionist, bookseller and copywriter and has almost finished her first novel.

Caitlin Ingham was born in 1990 and grew up in London and then Yorkshire. She studied English Literature at Queen Mary, University of London before spending two years working for a literary agency. In September 2014, she moved to Norwich to complete the Masters degree in Creative Writing (Prose) at UEA.

Adina Levay is one of Hungary's leading theatre directors. She was visiting director at three leading repertory companies in the country: New Theatre, Budapest, the National Theatre in Miskolc in Hungary and the Jokai Theatre, in Komarno, Slovakia, where she became Artistic Director. Since coming to the UK, Adina founded and became the Producing Artistic Director of Chalk Circle, a Norwich based small-scale theatre, and has produced and directed '4.48 Psychosis' at and in partnership with The Garage in Norwich, as well as 'We Lost Elijah', by Ryan Craig, a joint project with The Garage for the National Theatre Connections Festival, and the Contemporary European Drama Review.

Tess Little studied history at the Universities of Oxford and Cambridge, and is currently a Fellow of All Souls College, Oxford. Her research focused on les femmes tondues – French women punished after the Liberation for collaborating with Germans in the Second World War. During her studies, Tess wrote articles for student publications, and her short story 'The Stitches' was published in a student anthology. She's worked as a freelance journalist and previously gained experience at the *New York Times* in Paris, Ralph Appelbaum Associates in New York and Thomson Reuters in London.

Jane Martin has written several plays and loads of short pieces. In her mid-twenties, she abandoned creativity for academia gaining a BA in Eng. Lit. and an MA in Children's Lit, as well as a A levels in Psychology and Film Studies. She is now working with the Golden Egg Academy on honing her second children's novel.

Holly J. McDede claims to be a 10th generation King's Lynn resident in order to fit in, but really she moved to Norwich almost three years ago from California for secret reasons. She runs a radio show called the Norfolk Storytelling Project, where she explores hot topics such as zebra crossings, English banana farming, and public toilet facilities in Hailsham.

Anna Metcalfe was born in Holzwickede in 1987. Her stories have been published in *Tender Journal, Elbow Room, Lighthouse* and *The Warwick Review*. In 2014, she was shortlisted for The Sunday Times Short Story Award. She lives in Norwich, where she is working on her first collection.

Marise Mitchell lives in Dereham and teaches ESOL locally . She's written one novel, 'Bunny Slayer', published by YouWriteOn, and now has two books on the go: one a young adult fiction book set within a parallel universe and the other a collection of musings on the menopause as there is chick-lit and misery-lit but no menopause -lit out there!

Anthea Morrison grew up in Hertfordshire and has lived in London, Cambridge and New York, where she first realised her passion for creative writing at the Gotham Writers' Workshop. Now back in Cambridge, she is an active member of the local Angles writing workshop. Anthea has had stories published online, and is studying for an MA in Creative Writing at Royal Holloway University.

Patricia Mullin was shortlisted for an Arts Council Escalator Award in 2009. Her 2005 novel 'Gene Genie' was republished as an e–book in 2012, and 'The Sitting', a short story, was selected for *Words And Women: One*, published in 2014. Her novel 'Casting Shadows' was commended in the Yeovil International Literary prize 2014 and Patricia has just been awarded an Arts Council grant to re-draft 'Casting Shadows'.

Radhika Oberoi is pursuing an MA in Creative Writing (Prose Fiction) from the University of East Anglia. She is the recipient of an Asia Bursary, supported by the UEA Guardian Masterclasses. She is from India and has moonlighted as a journalist for the *Times of India*, the *Hindu Literary Review*, and more recently, the *New York Times* blog, *India Ink*.

Julianne Pachico grew up in Colombia and now lives in Norwich, where she is completing her PhD in Creative and Critical Writing at UEA. Her stories have been published or are forthcoming in *Lighthouse Literary Journal*, *NewWriting.net* and Salt's *Best British Short Stories*. Her pamphlet, 'The Tourists', is available with Daunt Books. She is currently completing a linked collection set in Colombia and working on a novel set in Mexico.

Sarah Ridgard is a graduate of the University of East Anglia with an MA in Creative Writing. She won a place on the Escalator Literature programme run by the Writers Centre Norwich in 2009, and three years later went on to publish her debut novel, 'Seldom Seen', with Random House. The novel was longlisted for the Desmond Elliott Prize 2013 for new fiction, the New Angle Prize for Literature and shortlisted for the Authors' Club Best First Novel Award. Sarah lives in Norwich and is currently working on her second novel.

Bethany Settle has an MA in Creative Writing (Prose Fiction) from the University of East Anglia. She remained in Norwich, where she works at a library. Reading, writing and nature are her top three best things. Recently her work has appeared in *Words and Women: One* and *Extending Leylines*. She is writer-in-residence at the Rumsey Wells pub in Norwich.

Avani Shah was born in London and now lives in Norwich. She has a BA in English Literature with Creative Writing from the University of East Anglia. Her influences include Jhumpa Lahiri, J.K. Rowling, and Mindy Kaling.

Thea Smiley lives in Suffolk with her husband and three sons. She graduated from the UEA in 2012 with a first class Honours Degree in English Literature. While at university, her short story 'Smoke' was published in *Workshop*, an anthology of undergraduate writing. Her first stage play was performed at the Cut Arts Centre, Halesworth, in 2012 and, the following year, one of her stories was shortlisted for the Bridport Prize. Currently, she is writing a play for Wonderful Beast Theatre Company, which will be performed during the HighTide Festival in 2015.

Lora Stimson studied creative writing at Norwich School of Art & Design and UEA. She's published stories and poems with *Nasty Little Press*, *Unthank Books*, *Ink, Sweat and Tears* and *Streetcake Magazine*. In 2014 she was mentored by novelist Shelley Harris as part of the WoMentoring scheme. Her first novel, about sex, grief and model villages, currently hides in a drawer. She has higher hopes for her second novel, about twins, which received an Arts Council England grant and is now in its final edit. Lora works as a programme manager for Writers' Centre Norwich and sings with the bands Moonshine Swing Seven and The Ferries.

Hannah Jane Walker is an award-winning poet, scriptwriter and producer. Her poems are full of sharp edges and unexpected angles as well as warmth and empathy for fellow humans. With collaborator Chris Thorpe she has made the shows 'The Oh Fuck Moment' and ˜I Wish I Was Lonely'. Hannah's extensively toured nationally and internationally, had plays and poems published by *Oberon Books*, *Penned in the Margins* and *Nasty Little Press* among others, and has written for *The Guardian*.

Lightning Source UK Ltd.
Milton Keynes UK
UKOW04f0253160515

251660UK00002B/40/P